# A Herd of Deer

# A Herd of Deer

by *Eilís Dillon*

*Illustrated by Richard Kennedy*

FUNK & WAGNALLS
NEW YORK

First published in the United States, 1970, by
Funk & Wagnalls, *A Division of* Reader's Digest Books, Inc.

Library of Congress Catalogue Card Number: 72–100651

Printed in the United States of America

1

A Herd of Deer

# 1

I FIRST MET MICHAEL JOYCE in Galway town. I was standing outside Powell's shop, holding a copy of the *Connacht Tribune* in my hands and peering anxiously at the advertisements. I suppose I must have looked anxious too because Mr. Joyce's first words were:

"What is worrying you so much on this fine afternoon?"

I had hardly noticed that it was a fine afternoon. It was June, the fifteenth to be precise, and the air was dry and clear and warm. In the narrow street, a procession of donkey and horse carts moved down from the square where there had been a cattle fair that morning. The men walking by the animals' heads were slouching tiredly. The women sat patiently on the corners of the carts with their feet, still in boots, dangling. Outside the town, the older ones would get the boots off and go the rest of the way home in comfort.

On the footpath, the Aran men moved slowly, looking judicially at the shop windows all glittering to entice them. They were easily recognizable by their tweed suits and by their rawhide shoes. The Connemara people were brisker. In fact they would knock you right off the path if you were not careful. The women carried huge baskets under their shawls, so that each woman took up the space of two. The men all carried sticks which they held trailing behind them like tails, and which were likely to trip up the person following them. The carts clanked in the dry air and the men yelled to each other cheerfully enough, as if they had had a profitable day.

I had no love for these people at that time. I had spent the whole morning rambling around the town. I had been to the potato market, in the part known as The West, where there were little eating-houses in which the country people could have tea. I had not a penny to my name, and my first dislike of the place may have come from the sight of those comfortable-looking people slowly chewing their way through hundreds of slices of soda-bread and butter. The few I spoke to answered me rough and short, so that I did not stay long there.

When I left the potato market I went to the fish market by the roaring, galloping Corrib River. After that I went through narrow streets to the market in the triangle below St. Nicholas' Cathedral, where eggs and vegetables and china were sold. There a woman silently handed me a double slice of bread and butter, having seen me watching her eat, I suppose. I hadn't wanted to take it.

"Go on," she said. "You're hungry. Why wouldn't you take a bite when you get it?"

She had a tiny donkey, and some eggs and cabbage and carrots to sell. She watched me eat and then she said, "Where are you from?"

"From Leitrim, ma'am—a long way."

"Up north somewhere?"

"Yes."

"Did you walk?"

"Not all the way."

"Are your people in Leitrim?"

"My mother only."

"You want work?"

"Yes."

"What kind of work?"

"Anything I can do well."

"Good on you. That's the right answer." She reached behind her onto the cart, where there was a tin box with money in it, and held out two pennies to me. "Go on take them," she said as I hesitated. "Amn't I old enough to be your mother? Go up there to Powell's shop, opposite the Munster and Leinster Bank, and buy the *Connacht Tribune*. On the back page you'll see a list of advertisements—maybe you've looked at them already?"

"No. I just asked a few people near the potato market." I felt hot as I remembered. "Some of them laughed at me and some of them pretended they didn't hear me."

" 'Twas bad manners out of them," she said. "In that part of Galway they have only enough work for themselves. But they could have told you where to go. There's plenty of work for everyone now, thanks be to God, especially if you're young and strong. Off with you now, and the blessings of God on you."

She told me her name was Nora Flaherty, and she lived in Furbo, six miles west of the town.

I went through the market, threading my way between the carts, in the direction she had pointed out. I had been sparing in my answers to Nora Flaherty. It was true that I came from Leitrim and that my mother was there, but I was glad not to have to explain how I came to be in Galway hungry and without a penny in my pocket.

The fact was that I was supposed to spend the summer in Roscommon with a cousin of my mother's, who had a sheep farm there. This was my mother's idea, but I had no liking for that man. My mother did not know it, but every time he came to our house, he found an opportunity of saying to me that I was a spoiled mother's boy and that a taste of real work on his land would do me a power of good. So when school finished and my innocent mother put me on the bus for Roscommon, I just could not bring myself to go there. Looking back on it now, this seems very wicked, but it did not seem too bad at the time.

From Roscommon to Galway is the best part of forty miles

and I had to walk most of the way. I slept in a barn the first night and in an out building the second as the weather was fine, and the last night I spent with a camp of gypsies—tinkers we call them.

I should have known better than to trust those gentry. It was coming on for dark, with a spatter of rain, and a little whining wind. I was on a desolate part of the road with not a house in sight. I was getting braver by this time and I think I would have asked for shelter in a house if I had seen a lighted window.

But the only light came from the tinkers' fire, low on the roadside. They were camped on a triangle of grass where a side road joined the one that I was on. They had three tents, one of a good size and two smaller ones. A little distance away, a donkey was grazing the roadside grass, tethered to the shaft of his own cart which stood tilted with its tail in the air.

The tinkers had a big turf fire and the light from it glowed on their faces as they sat in a ring around it. They were roasting potatoes, turning them in the ashes with long, pointed sticks. There were seven or eight of them—I was never able to count the children as they kept moving in and out of the firelight.

The father was a short, broad man who moved as fast as a goat. The mother was thin and red-haired, and she had the sharp eyes and nose of a fox. I could not help comparing them with animals, though I knew it was an unchristian thought. The ease with which they lived out under the wide sky had something to do with it. The children were like rabbits, and if you think rabbits are innocent, pretty creatures, you have never owned a country vegetable garden.

I thought afterward that they had seen me coming a long way off and had arranged themselves as hospitably as possible. As I walked toward them in the dusk, I could not take my eyes off the glowing fire. When I came level with them, the mother called out softly, "Good night to you, boy."

"Good night," I said uncertainly.

13 ✍

The father said, "Where would you be going this hour of the night?"

"To Galway."

"That's a long way," said the mother. "Where are you going to sleep?"

"I don't know."

"You must find a lodging. It's a long, cold road," she said, "and not many houses."

"I could keep walking," I said, though I did not enjoy the prospect.

"Then you're braver than we are," she said. "I wouldn't walk this road at night. The ghosts of the men of Aughrim ride this road every night, so they say."

They all looked at me solemnly, and I shivered at the
thought. The great Battle of Aughrim was lost in the moment
of victory and was one of the saddest stories in the history of
Ireland. I could well imagine that the ghosts of the vanquished
army would patrol the whole area forever after, stopping unfortunate travelers to tell them all about it.

I took one step toward the warm, cheerful fire. Instantly the
father said, "You're welcome and more than welcome to stay
with us. One more is always welcome. Move over, there," he
said to the children, "and make room for the honest man. We
are the Burkes," he explained to me. "Everyone knows us.
You're in good hands. In a few minutes the potatoes will be
ready roasted and we'll have a feast fit for a king."

So I sat down among them. They had some sausages too, which they held on their sticks over the red embers until they turned a heavenly brown. We had several each, and they went perfectly with the potatoes. No one spoke much. In fact I thought they were the quietest family I had ever sat with. The children moved in and out of the circle around the fire like shadows, and as night fell, one by one they crept into the smaller tents and were seen no more.

I was dead tired after my several days' walking. Soon I began to yawn, and the father said gently, "Into our tent with you and stretch yourself out. Potatoes and sausages bring on a powerful sleep. We'll sit here a while in the quietness."

So I went into the big tent and lay on some straw that they had spread out. Between the walking, the potatoes, the turf smoke, and the heat, in a few minutes I was enjoying the deepest sleep of my life.

When I awoke in the morning, the strength of the sunlight almost blinded me. That was only for a second. Suddenly I sat up. I was quite alone. The tents and the tinkers were gone. Their donkey and cart had disappeared too. All that remained to prove that I had not dreamed it was the heap of ash where the fire had been and the straw on which I was lying, as open to the weather as a cow in a field.

I put my hand in my jacket pocket, but I knew I would find it empty. The little store of money I had had was gone silently with the tinkers. I felt suddenly weak, and above all very foolish. How could I ever have trusted them? It was the warm, inviting fire that had made me forget their reputation. By now they would be hours away, I thought bitterly. I could not help feeling a little admiration for the stealth and speed with which they had slipped the tent from above my body.

This feeling only lasted for a second. As I walked the rest of the way to Galway, I promised myself every kind of revenge on them if I were ever to catch up with them. I would know them anywhere, as long as I lived.

My breakfast was a piece of bread which had been left for me on the straw. As I brushed the beetles off it, I wondered which of them had thought of that. It was not much, and was long forgotten by the time I reached the town.

Perhaps it was unreasonable of me to blame the people of Galway for a misfortune which I had certainly brought on myself. It was not surprising that they did not like me, with my glaring eyes and surly manners. When I turned to Mr. Joyce and glowered at him from under my eyebrows, he stepped back in mock terror and said, "Don't eat me!"

As I was thinking unceasingly of food, this made me give a sour laugh. I looked him up and down and said, "I almost would."

"Come along and I'll give you something more palatable," he said. "Then we can talk about why you're looking so hard at that newspaper."

He took me into a nearby restaurant and ordered bacon and eggs, tea, and bread and butter and cakes. He watched me while I ate, so that I had to go slowly for decency's sake. He said very little, except to urge me to finish everything on the table. At last there was no single corner of me that was not satisfied and I leaned back in my chair with a sense of enormous gratitude.

"Now we can talk," he said. "My name is Michael Joyce. What is yours?"

"Peter Regan."

"How old are you?"

"Fifteen."

"You want work. I saw you reading the advertisements in the paper."

"Yes."

"What are you able to do?"

"Farming work."

I said this reluctantly. It was true that it was the only real skill I had, from working for our neighbors at home after school since my father died. But I knew it for badly paid, laborious work and I had hopes of getting something to do which would be more profitable.

"You don't sound happy at the idea."

I looked at him more closely. Until now, I had been busy looking at my food, and I had not really examined my host at all. He was a tall, thin man with grayish hair, perhaps fifty years old. His skin was tanned by an open-air life and he had the alert look of an outdoor man, but he was not dressed like any rich farmer that I had ever seen. He wore a dark blue suit of a beautiful cut. I said suddenly, "You're not an Irishman, in spite of your name."

"How do you know?"

"Your clothes, your accent—"

"No one would take me for an Irishman?"

"No."

He sighed and said, "You're quite right, of course. I was born in Argentina, though my father was an Irishman from Galway County. He said that that made an Irishman of me. Now tell me why you don't want to work on a farm."

"I want to learn a lot of things," I said, while at the back of my mind was a feeling of surprise that I should tell these thoughts to anyone. "In Ireland, everyone must stay at school until he's fourteen years old. After that he can go to work, or he can go to another school. When I was fourteen, I should have gone to work, but the teacher came to our house to talk to my mother and he persuaded her to let me stay at the elementary school another year. He said there were lots of things he could teach me still. There was no secondary school in our district. She agreed when she found that I wanted it, and I went back, but I felt foolish, sitting at a desk with people younger than me, though I was learning different things. I stayed for most of the year, but I knew before the end of it that I wouldn't be able to stay a second year."

"So you left home to find work?"

Then I told him the story of my cousin who had the sheep farm and how I had hoped to do better for myself than that, and save my money to get some more learning in a school for people of my own age. Not even to my mother had I said anything about my hopes. The fine meal I had just finished, and the strange surroundings, but above all Mr. Joyce's kindly face had drawn it all out of me.

"So I need work until the end of August," I said. "There's talk of a new school being opened about six miles from us. If I have a bit saved, I'll be able to persuade my mother to let me go there. The school is free, but we have to live as well."

I hardly dared to believe in the new school, though I knew well that it was real. The walls of it had been roof high three months ago and all our neighbors said that it was promised to be opened in September.

Mr. Joyce was watching me. Now he said, "Why do you want so much to go to school again? To get a good job at the end of it?"

"I haven't thought of that yet," I said in surprise. "I want to learn Latin and Greek and French and German and Russian—"

"Easy, easy!" he said, as if he were talking to a frisky horse. "Will they teach all those languages in that school?"

This was another thing that I had not thought of, but I said, "They'll teach some of them anyway."

He asked suddenly and sharply, "Would you like to work for me?"

"Yes." As an afterthought I asked, "What sort of work?"

"I hardly know how to answer that," he said. "I just know that I need help." He paused and looked at me steadily for a few seconds, as if he were estimating the possibility of my understanding him. Then he went on, "All the time while I was growing up, my father was talking about Ireland and the beautiful country of Connemara. Long before I saw it, I knew what the sunset was like there, and how the moon looks over a calm

19 🖋

sea on a summer's night. I knew about the smell of a turf fire, and how the people sit in the evenings telling stories about the great heroes of long ago.

"So when I was able, I left the country where I was born and came to Ireland, and I bought a house and some land in Connemara so that I could enjoy those things myself."

"Where is your house and land?"

"Twenty miles west of the town, eight miles or so beyond Spiddal. Some of my land runs down to the sea, but the house is in a hollow, a little way inland."

"It's not very good land, from all I've ever heard of that part of the country."

"That's true, and that is the cause of my trouble. I could see at once that it was no use trying to farm as I always used to do—a few hundred acres of wheat, a few hundred cattle, a few hundred horses."

"You could not, indeed," I said with a sour laugh. "The people would be shocked to think of one man owning all those animals." I was rather shocked myself.

Mr. Joyce said, "But I thought it out and I realized that there is one kind of animal that could live in that place, that doesn't eat much grass, that's hardy enough to stand the winter, and that was quite at home in Ireland in the old times. Deer and stags come into all the old stories. So I bought a little herd of deer from a Scotsman and I put them on my land."

"When?"

"Last September. There were two two-year-old roebucks and three yearlings, and twenty does and their fawns. I had them shipped in to Galway straight from Glasgow. They caused quite a stir when they were landed on the docks. I hired a Scottish herdsman with them, because he knows how to look after them. They seem to know him too. He has names for them all, and they come like dogs when he calls them.

"Last week he told me that one of the two-year-old bucks and three does are missing. At first I wouldn't take it seriously.

I thought they might have gone up to the high part of the land, and of course with their coloring, it's almost impossible to see them until you're close. But he said he had searched everywhere. He has two dogs that he takes with him, and he walked every inch of the land without finding them."

"How much land have you got?"

"Not too much. Less than seven hundred acres."

It seemed after all that there were some things his father had not told him. I could imagine how the Connemara people would feel toward this rich foreigner with his herd of deer and his huge kingdom of land, while they struggled to make a living out of twenty or thirty acres and a fishing boat, with perhaps a Government pension to keep off the worst of the winter's hunger.

As if he knew what I was thinking, he said, "The Scotsman asked a few questions—if anyone had seen the deer—but he could get no straight answers. And somehow the people don't seem as friendly to me as they used to be. They turn off the road and go into their houses or into a side road if they see me coming. They were not like that in the beginning. And I have no way of finding out what became of my deer until some Irishman will help me. I could send for the Civic Guards, of course, but afterward how could I ever be friendly with my neighbors again?"

"You could not, indeed. Perhaps the deer have wandered."

"I don't think so. I've seen what happens when an animal wanders. Within an hour or two, someone comes along to the owner and says, 'I saw your cows out on the strand a while back,' or, 'Your sow is gone off up the road toward Screeb. I sent young Johnny to fetch her back.' They even seem to know the sheep apart."

I knew that he was right in this. It was the same in my part of the country. With an animal as remarkable as a deer, it would be quite impossible for it to wander off unnoticed.

Michael Joyce said, "You're an intelligent boy. You're well

grown for your age and you're in good health. It seems to me that if you were to come to my district, you would find out more in a day than I would hear in a month."

"If I sleep and eat in your house, I'll hear nothing."

"I have thought of that. That's why I said you should come to my *district,* and why I made the comment about your health. Have you ever slept in a tent?"

"I did it last night," I said, and I told him about my night in the Burkes' encampment which was the reason for my penniless state.

"Did you sleep well?"

"Never better. That was my trouble."

"Then what I propose is this: I will buy you a little tent and everything that an energetic boy would need on a camping holiday. In a day or two, you can walk to my place and pitch your tent, make friends with everyone, and find out for me what has happened. If you get back my deer alive and well, I'll give you a hundred pounds into your hand the day you leave me."

The sum was staggering. I tried not to look as surprised as I felt.

"And if I don't find your deer?" I asked.

"I'll give you fifty pounds, and the price of your food as long as you are working for me. That will be for any information you will get."

He watched me closely while I thought it over. There was nothing dishonest in what I was asked to do. It was quite true that he and his Scotsman could live in that place until the crack of doom and never hear a straight answer to a straight question. This was not surprising. For many centuries we Irish have developed a habit of secrecy with strangers, especially with English-speaking strangers from a foreign country. But it seemed to me that Michael Joyce had a right to know what had become of his deer and that if by accepting the work of finding this out for him I were to keep the Civic Guards out of the business, I would be doing a good turn to his neighbors as well as to himself. In any case I hoped that there would prove to be some innocent explanation of the mystery. I said, "Very well. I'll come."

He took me at once to a big shop near Eyre Square, where he bought me a dark green canvas tent, a ground sheet, and a sleeping bag, as well as a tiny stove and a cooking pot. He examined each of these articles carefully, in a way that showed he had experience of them in use. He bought a special set of wooden pegs, instead of the light metal ones supplied with the tent by the manufacturers, and he said to me, "They're heavier to carry, but you'll be glad of them if a wind comes up. Have you ever thought of camping out before?"

"No," I said. "I think it's a sport for city people. I'd need to have a reason to sleep out if I could be in a house."

"Then you had better give out that you're from some big town. What is the nearest one to your home?"

"Sligo is not far away."

"Have you been there?"

"Yes."

"Then Sligo it is. What is the river in Sligo called?"

"The Garavogue."

"And the lake?"

"Lough Gill."

"And the mountains?"

"Ben Bulben and Knocknarea. The grave of Queen Maeve of Connacht is on top of Ben Bulben."

"Good. But don't get into too much talk about it unless you're sure of your ground."

We left the things to be packed into a rucksack. The tent could be rolled up neatly and it had some straps of its own which could be attached to the rucksack. Then we went to buy a few stores. Porridge was good camping food, Mr. Joyce said, and could be eaten hot or cold. Sausages and bacon were quick to cook and buying them gave you a reason to go into the country shops where all the news was usually passed around. Getting milk and eggs was useful in the same way, and

I should try to visit farmhouses rather than shops for these things. Then he gave me five one-pound notes and some advice on where to camp.

"Never pitch your tent on ferns. They're full of ticks which will get under your skin while you sleep and torment the life out of you. Moss is not good, though it looks so soft, because as well as being damp, it's often full of ants. If you find an earwig in the tent, better put him out than kill him, because he gives off a nasty smell in revenge. It's enough to turn a beetle's head toward the door—he'll walk out, ten chances to one. Don't camp under trees, because if it rains, the leaves will drip on your tent for hours afterward. Thick grass is bad for the reason that it's slow to dry after rain. Don't camp in the path of the wind, or you may wake up to find your tent gone—as happened when you were with the tinkers."

"Then where can I camp?" I asked in dismay.

"In a hollow, on short, thin grass, but not on sandy ground. Sand won't hold your pegs. In a long hollow, to one end, on a slight slope but not too much, or when it rains the water from above will run through your tent. Near a wall, if you like, but not too near because the wind hitting the wall would rebound on you. And don't go too near the sea. A hollow field close to the sea could fill up with water at the spring tide. And another thing: keep away from haystacks and from big stacks of straw. They give good shelter, but in warm, damp weather a haystack can go on fire by itself, and no farmer alive would believe you hadn't put a match to it."

By this time, as you can imagine, I had formed the idea that I would never find a safe place to camp. If I escaped the ticks, I would surely come on the ants; and if I avoided the wind, I would be burned alive in a haystack. However, I could not help feeling a sense of excitement at the notion of living for a while as the tinkers do, free in time and place and movement.

This thought reminded me to make one resolution of my own, not to camp in the tinkers' regular places. I could imagine how they would feel toward an interloper and how they would envy me my fancy equipment. It would be easy to identify the tinkers' camping places by the pieces of tin and the old cans and bottles, and always for some reason little heaps of rags of every color.

Mr. Joyce gave me an exact description of the position of his house.

"But you must not come there, of course," he said. "A quarter of a mile to the west of it there is a low cliff, half-turned to the sea. You can't miss it. On the eastern side of that you will find an old shepherd's hut, a sort of dugout in the side of the hill. I often walk up there in the evenings to look at the sea, and two or three days from now, I'll hope to find you there. But take your time. Get used to your way of living. In that way you will seem to have been doing it for a few weeks at least by the time you come to my place."

"Where will I meet you?"

"You can wait inside the hut until I come. No one ever goes there."

"Suppose the owner takes a notion to walk up there just when we meet?"

He laughed and said, "He will. I am the owner."

Carrying my stores, we walked back to the other shop. My tent was ready packed, and when I had put the food into the rucksack, Mr. Joyce and the shop assistant harnessed me into it. The assistant was not more than a few years older than myself. He looked at me with envy as I strutted about, getting the feel of the unaccustomed weight on my shoulders. When I came back to the counter, he said softly, "You're lucky to have such a father."

"I agreed, though I thought he might have wondered how such an elegant father could have such a scruffy son. I had slept in my clothes for several nights, and washing without soap in streams does not do much for one.

Mr. Joyce had not failed to notice this. As we came out of the shop, he said, "Your clothes are at your cousin's place, I suppose."

"Yes."

"You'll need a shirt or two, at least. And some more suitable boots for walking. Otherwise you won't look like a man of leisure."

"Wait," I said. "How do you know that when you're gone west I won't just turn east with all my new finery and never see you again?"

He looked me up and down with a humorous eye and then said, "You won't. You won't do that at all."

He seemed so sure of this that when he left me later I did not hesitate for as much as a minute's thinking before starting out on my long walk to the west.

# ❧ 2

I LEFT GALWAY BY THE fish market. As I passed through it, there was no sign of the crowd that had been there in the morning. Only the seagulls howled and squalled over the cleanings that had been left for them to deal with. As I crossed the Wolfe Tone Bridge I looked back at the Cathedral clock. It was half-past five, a bad time of the day, it seemed to me, to be setting out on such a pilgrimage.

I took the road through the Claddagh and along by the sea, not because I knew the way but because the sun gave me my direction. The sea was silky calm, pale blue as far as the horizon. The mountains of Clare in the distance were a darker blue, flecked here and there with brilliant white. Quite close to the shore there was an island with a tall, white lighthouse. Off in the distance, three dim curves of varying sizes I took to be the Aran Islands. It was my first sight of Galway Bay and I thought that it must be the most beautiful place in the whole world.

Presently I came to Salthill, where there were rows of hotels all shined up and ready for the summer people. My mother had told me that her grandmother and her great-aunts had always come here long ago, for two weeks' summer holiday. She had come with them once when she was young, but she had laughed so much that they would never take her again. She could not help it, she said, when she saw them drinking the sea water out of pint mugs and later complaining of the stomach-ache. They had had lodgings opposite the sea front, in a tiny street with the horrid name of Flea Lane. Here the holiday people slept in rows on the floor of the kitchen, in relays. One lot would lie down from nine o'clock in the evening until three o'clock in the morning, when they gave place to the second lot who slept until nine. The women were all wives of strong farm-ers from inland places. Each woman brought her own frying pan, and she could have water from the big communal kettle to make tea. She could also boil her potatoes in the common pot. Short of sleep, crowded together, half-poisoned with drinking sea water, they still would not have missed their an-nual holiday for the world and said that it set them up for the whole winter.

I looked for Flea Lane but supposed that it would not have been named in this way on a signboard.

My new boots were comfortable, but I was very tired of walking. Occasionally a late cart would clatter past, going at a trot, and I longed to ask for a lift. Instead I kept gazing out at the sea as if I were enjoying it too much to take my eyes off it. I was reluctant to start telling my story, knowing that I would have to answer a lot of searching questions. Besides, I was not in such a hurry to reach Michael Joyce's place. It seemed to me that he had given me good advice when he had said I should become used to this way of life first. It had occurred to me that my tent and other equipment looked very new, and that if I were to arouse suspicion in any way, this would be held in evidence against me.

Still I walked for more than an hour before stopping for the night. After the hotels, the town ended. The road turned a little inland and there was first a golf course and then green fields with scattered houses, some of them very new and grand. Then I went up a long hill and came to a cross where the road forked. The right-hand road clearly led back to the town, and the road to the left led out to the west.

As I turned along this road, I smelled the sea again—a wild, strong smell with a salty tang in it, which I later came to know very well. I knew that there were hours of daylight before me still, as is always the way in Ireland in the middle of June. Still, I decided to find a camping place soon, since I suspected that I would be awkward at putting up the tent for the first time.

Now I could see how the land sloped gently down toward the sea. Down there, it seemed there was a sort of tidal lake, with a bar of land between it and the sea. With Michael Joyce's advice all jumbled about in my head, I began to work out whether it would be better for me to camp on the sea or on the land side of the road.

What finally decided me was the thought of the Burkes. On the landward side, the ground sloped uphill so that anyone pitching a tent there would be visible from a long way off. It occurred to me that if the Burkes happened to come by, as they very easily might, they would see an opportunity for acquiring a brand-new tent. By now they knew what a heavy sleeper I was, and I could imagine how they would wait so silently until I would be asleep and then come sneaking up to unhook the roof over my head as they had done before. This thought haunted me for the rest of the night.

Very soon I came to a short avenue leading downhill to a comfortable two-story farmhouse. Trees sheltered it, and though I knew there must be a field behind the house, the view of it was cut off by the trees and by the house itself. They were low, salt-bitten trees, but just now they were in full leaf.

The front of the house was covered in pink cabbage roses, and beds of wallflowers grew close against it at either side of the door. Slow bees droned in and out of the flowers. Through the open door I could see right into the kitchen, where the farmer and his wife and three little boys were sitting at their supper. The kettle was humming gently over the turf fire. A stout tabby cat was curled on the hearth, as close as he dared to the hot ashes. A plain wooden staircase led to the rooms above. There were pictures on the walls, and a clock with a pendulum, and a little lamp in front of the holy statue. It was such a beautiful, warm scene that it seemed to me a hard thing to have to lie on the ground under the weather, with nothing between me and heaven but a piece of cloth, while other people enjoyed such solid comfort.

However, I put these self-pitying thoughts away from me and tried to remember Michael Joyce's valuable deer. I went to the door, diffidently enough, and asked if I might camp in the field behind the house.

"You can and welcome," said the farmer. "I'll come down with you. Are you all alone?"

"Yes."

"Won't you be lonesome during the night?" his wife asked. "Do you stay out like that alone always?"

"I won't be lonesome," I said. "I'm used to it."

"Listen to that, Patcheen!" she said to one of the children. "Why aren't you as brave as that?" She turned back to me. "Imagine it, Patcheen is eleven years old and he wants the light in his room all night. A candle, too, that might set the house on fire."

Patcheen glared, and I said quickly, "I wanted the light until I was twelve years old, and then I got over it."

She was not pleased with that as it had spoiled her lesson, but Patcheen was delighted. He came with me and his father to show me the place where I might camp.

It was a perfect place, answering all of Michael Joyce's specifications—a sloping field, sheltered by the barns of the farmyard and by a low wood which ran right down to the sea. The grass was short and clean.

The farmer said, "The cows are all in the other field, beyond the house. They were in here until last week. If the dogs come around, don't take any notice of them. Patcheen will show you the well."

And he went off to his cows, leaving Patcheen with me. He was a friendly boy, smart with his hands, and I was very glad of his help in putting up the tent. Of course he thought that I was an old hand at this, but in reality it was through his questions that I learned how to do it.

"Do you lay it out on the ground first? Do you put in the poles and get the tent up on them then? Do you start with a peg at the four corners first and put in the other ones afterward? Do you knock in the pegs at a slant, so that they won't come out easily? Do you fix these corner pegs again when it's all done, to pull it tight?"

He bobbed and danced around, holding the tent poles for me and stretching the guy ropes, so that we had it erected in half the time that it would have taken me alone. When we had spread the ground sheet inside, he went in and sat there. Then he lay full length, to try the feel of that.

"I'd love to be sleeping here with you," he said then. "But I'd be afraid."

"There's nothing to be afraid of."

"I'd be afraid of my mortal life," he said, "of lions and tigers and bears and pumas and ghosts and tinkers." He looked at me with envy. " 'Tis well for you, not to be afraid."

The last two things he had mentioned were the only ones I was afraid of. I said casually, "The tinkers have their own places. They don't come off the main road. And they won't come down here without leave."

"I suppose they won't," he said doubtfully.

I did not care to ask about the ghosts, for fear of what I might hear.

He showed me the well, and watched as I made porridge on my new stove. While it was cooking, he ran to get a bottle of milk from his mother, and she added a few slices of soda-bread with raisins in it.

Patcheen said as he watched me eat, "I never saw anyone eating porridge for their supper before, but it seems to me a fine thing to do."

After I had finished and had put away my things, he brought me to walk along the shore below the woods. It was a calm evening with a smooth sea. The sun went down while we walked there, and with a little splash a seal hauled himself up on a rock and sat resting himself. It began to turn cold. Patcheen said, "I must be going home. I'll come down to see you in the morning."

And he ran off through the wood. In the darkening evening I got back to my tent and unrolled my sleeping bag. It was warm enough when I had been inside it for a few minutes. The silence was broken only by the sighing noise of the sea. I lay on my back, with my eyes stretched wide and my ears, it seemed to me, grown long and pointed to catch every sound. At first there was nothing but the wash of the sea. Then, unmistakably, I heard a snuffing sound, quick and interested, coming closer every moment. Bears, lions, pumas—which would it be? I lay rigidly, unable to move. In fact I would have made an easy meal for any of those beasts if one had happened to come along.

A short, sharp bark revealed soon enough that these were the farmer's dogs of which he had warned me. They took a great interest in my tent, poking their noses under the front flap in the hope of getting in. I called out, "Go home!"

And a few seconds later they were gone. But I had had such a fright that it was hours before I could sleep. All around me I fancied I heard noises, of people approaching on stealthy feet, or of spirits from another world swishing their trailing draperies—the only sound they were allowed to make, as I had been told by a helpful friend at school.

Eventually, of course, from sheer exhaustion, I slept heavily. It was Patcheen who woke me in the morning, bringing me more fresh milk. He watched me eat the remains of my cold porridge and only then did he convey an invitation from his mother to come to the house for breakfast.

"I didn't bother asking you," he said. "I knew you'd like it better out here in the field."

He had certainly liked it better watching me eat squatting on the dewy grass than sitting tamely at a table like everyone else. He helped me to strike the tent and roll it up, and he watched me along the road for as far as he could see me when I went away.

It was another fine, sunny morning, with not a cloud in sight. Soon after I left my camping place, the character of the country changed. The fields were rocky and misshapen, and the lanes that led off the main road were twisty and rough underfoot. The land, if one could give it that name, was divided into irregularly shaped fields by stone walls of varying heights. The houses were mostly set back from the road, shining with whitewash after the spring cleaning. By comparison with the fine place where I had spent last night, however, houses and land were miserable here.

But the people were cheerful and friendly, as I soon found out. At Barna I stopped for a drink of water in a long, dark shop. Several men were drinking pints of black porter at the counter. They all turned to look at me, with the humorous eye to which I was going to become accustomed. They edged a little nearer when the woman behind the counter handed me a glass of water and said, "A fine day for walking."

I agreed that it was.

"You're going out west?"

"Yes."

"They're a bit wild out there," said one of the men solemnly.

"Ara, don't mind him," said another. "Where would you be from yourself?"

"From Leitrim," I said, before I remembered that it was to have been Sligo.

"Ah. The land is poor enough there, I've heard."

"It's not the worst."

"No. The worst is Connemara and no mistake. You're on a holiday?"

"Yes."

"Fine for you. Did you walk from Leitrim?"

"Yes."

" 'Tis a good walk. You must be fine and strong."

"Yes."

Since they were getting no information whatever out of me, they turned back to their drinks then, and I finished mine and went outside. I was burning with a sense of failure. Michael Joyce had told me to collect information in the shops as I passed by. I had imagined myself asking a series of clever questions, gradually picking out the things I wanted to know like snails out of their shells. It was clear to me now, however, that unless I changed my methods I would learn nothing. There was a little comfort in the thought that Barna was probably still too far from Michael Joyce's district for me to have found out anything useful.

A mile or so farther along, I saw in a cottage window some packets of soap and jars of sweets balanced against the glass. Beside the door was a familiar painted sign, green and gold, that said: "Wills Wild Woodbine Cigarettes." Above the door a tiny faded notice said: "Mary Fahy. Licensed to deal in Tobacco."

As I had guessed, the shop was just a counter running along one end of the kitchen. There was a fine turf fire with a pot of potatoes hanging on the crane above it. As I came in, a thin, sharp-faced woman lifted the pot down onto the floor.

"Let me strain it for you," I said quickly.

"The blessings of God on you," she said. "There's a basket outside the door for it. I don't know am I getting old or what, but that pot gets heavier every week, so it does."

I put my baggage in the corner of the kitchen and took up the pot. Outside the door I found a flat basket made of willow rods. I poured the contents of the pot into it, so that the boiling water ran away, and I was left with a steaming mound of floury potatoes. I carried this into the shop again and found that she had pulled out the table from the wall and had it all cleared for the basket to be laid in the middle. While the steam rose up to the rafters, she said, "Did you want to buy something?"

"Sausages and potatoes, if you have them," I said, and my mouth watered at the thought of them.

"For your dinner, is it?"

"Yes."   U. S. 1529913

"There would be no sense in that," she said. "I have a mountain of potatoes ready cooked, as you can see, and I'll give you a fine slice of bacon to go with it if you'll sit down and eat with me. All my men are up at the bog footing turf this fine day and I was going to be all alone. I'd be with them myself only for the shop. I do love a day on the bog."

This was a very welcome invitation, you may be sure. Already I was hungry, and it would be at least an hour before I would have had my own meal cooked, if I had refused.

We sat at either side of the table with the ridiculously big heap of potatoes between us. I accounted for about six of them and Mrs. Fahy had two or three. The rest, she said, were for her two voracious pigs which were in the little field behind the house. Long before we had finished, they had begun to howl for them, but she took no notice.

"On your holidays you are?" she said when we began to eat.

"Yes."

"Fine dry weather you have for it, though it won't stay dry forever. Which way would you be going?"

"Out west," I said. "If I find a place I like, maybe I'll stay there for a while."

" 'Tis well to be young. Doesn't your mother be afraid to let you sleep out alone?"

"She says fresh air is good."

This was true; indeed it was a great saying of hers always.

"She's right, of course. Were you ever in this part of the world before?"

"Never," I said. "It's beautiful country. I'd like to see the whole of it."

" 'Tis all right on a fine day," she said, "but we do get terrible storms here, winter and summer."

"Then I'll have to look out for sheltered places for my tent
or it will be blown away."

"Faith and it's not easy to find shelter in Connemara. That's
one thing we're always short of."

"Maybe I'll find a big barn full of hay and get to leeward of
it when the storm is coming up."

She laughed and said, "A barn! That's another thing we're
short of. And if we had a few, we wouldn't have much to put
into them. Life isn't the same here as it is where you come
from, I can see."

"There's turf stacks in plenty, though," I said.

"True for you. After you pass Salleen, there's one place only that I know of where you'll find a barn to shelter you. But you won't be needing that. Maybe no storm will come, and if it does, you can always sleep on the settle in someone's kitchen until it blows over."

Trying not to sound too curious, I asked her quietly, "Where is that barn? It might be no harm to know about it, anyway."

"Seven or eight miles beyond Salleen, maybe more," she said. "It's years since I had time to go for a jaunt out that way. It's a fine big house down from the road, and with sheds and barns every bit as big as it all around. It used to belong to Colman Donnelly, but he sold it to a foreigner last year. It's a fine place, but Colman hadn't the wits to mind it, and they say that when the foreigner offered him a big price for it, he jumped at it. It was Colman's father, God rest him, that had that place. His father bought it from some old English Colonel or Knight or Captain in the bad times. Old Donnelly had the best shop in all Connemara. You could buy anything there, from a shovel to a suit of clothes, and groceries of all kinds as well. After he made his money, he bought out his landlord for the satisfaction of it. Funny how those tough old raspers often have weedy sons."

I agreed that it was funny indeed.

"Colman never made anything of himself," she said with pity. "He got plenty of chances but it wasn't a bit of good. He was apprenticed to a fine shop in Galway—" she named the one where Michael Joyce had bought my tent—"but after a few months there, they sent him home. Then he used to be going fishing with the men, and rambling around the land shooting birds, but he never did a stroke of work. And the worst of all was when he went looking for a wife. There was many a fine, buxom girl from his own place that would have made a man of him, but in to Galway he went, and brought home a long thin one that hasn't a word of Irish and goes out all dressed up as if she was on the streets of New York instead of in the back of Connemara."

I felt a twinge of sympathy for the long thin one, who had carried off this doubtful prize from under the noses of the local girls. It sounded as if Colman Donnelly was what used to be called a "half-Sir," one who could not easily be placed in any social category. He was neither poor nor rich, neither a shop-keeper nor a farmer, neither educated nor ignorant. In fact he was a thorn in everyone's flesh, and probably a worry to their consciences too, since no one could really make friends with him. But it seemed that he had had the sense not to marry a girl who would spoil his easy way of life by making a man of him.

"A fine quarter of land he had," Mrs. Fahy was saying, "the best for miles around, and a fine house. He could have made a fortune there. The way he is now, he'll be watching his money to see will it last as long as himself."

"What became of the shop?" I asked.

"He never liked the shop," said Mrs. Fahy. "I don't blame him. A shop is like a bed-ridden granny—you can't leave it for as much as an hour. The minute his father died, he sold off everything and closed it all up, and the door is shut ever since. It's hard on the people around that part. Their boots are worn out from walking to the next shop a couple of miles farther on, I'm told. There's a little shop like mine, where you can buy flour and soap and a few sweets, but not a pair of boots or a shovel or anything useful like that. They keep a few barrels of porter too, but it's nothing like Donnelly's used to be."

At this point our conversation was interrupted by a child with three eggs carefully carried in both hands, to be ex-changed for their value in bread-soda. When she had gone out with her little packet, I said, "Perhaps the new owner will start a shop one of these days."

"Faith and he won't," Mrs. Fahy said. "By what I've heard of him, he won't do anything ordinary. You'd never guess what he has on his land—and it isn't cows or sheep or horses either."

"Lions? Tigers?"

"You're not far out. A herd of deer! Did you ever hear the beat of that? I've never been out there myself, as I told you, but I've heard that they're prancing around as if they owned the place. A man that would think of keeping such a queer class of an animal won't be likely to be satisfied with a shop."

When I gathered up my baggage at last, I felt that I had not wasted my time on this occasion. As Mrs. Fahy said, she had all her information at second-hand, but surely if she had heard of the disappearance of some of the deer, she would have spoken of it. I could not ask her any questions about this, without letting her see that the existence of the deer had not been news to me.

Before leaving her, I bought half a pound of sausages and some bread and butter for my supper.

"And if you're walking back this way in a few weeks' time, you can call in and we'll have a chat," she said. "And you can bring me all the news."

After a while I came to a broad beach with long fingers of rock at either side to shelter it. The tide was coming in over the warm sand, but the water was still stinging cold after the winter, as I found when I waded into it. Afterward I had to run up and down the beach to get warm. At one end, close to the reef, there was a collection of tiny jewellike shells, laid out like a carpet, all the colors of the rainbow.

Not far from the beach there was a stunted wood and a big house on the side of the road away from the sea. After that, there were little fields again and thatched houses until I came near a big village. By this time it was late afternoon. I had rested often and I had spent a long time over my swim, so that I was ravenously hungry again. My legs felt suddenly weak, and the tent and knapsack seemed to have doubled in weight since morning. Off in front of me I could see a cluster of houses

and a gray church spire. From what Mrs. Fahy had said, I
guessed that this must be Salleen. That meant that there were
still eight miles to go before I would reach Michael Joyce's
land.

There could be no question of getting there this evening.
With my small experience, putting up my tent in the dark
would be an impossibility. Besides, I felt that there was some
hope of picking up a little information in Salleen, as it was not
so far from Michael Joyce's house.

At the place where I was, the road had taken a little turn
inland, so that the sea was perhaps a quarter of a mile away.

To the sea side of the road, there was a fine stone house with a slate roof. It stood on a little rise of ground, and though there was a clean, grassy field beside it, I thought of Michael Joyce's advice and decided that it would be too exposed for me.

To my right, on the landward side, there was a little wood of sycamore and birch, with a clearing visible from the road. The road wall was close built and would shelter me from the sea wind. The clearing was gently sloped toward a small stream.

While I was looking around me, a man came out of the house and walked deliberately as far as his boundary wall. I waited for him, while he got out his pipe and lit it, and while he took two or three comfortable pulls. Then I took a step toward him. He sighed with satisfaction at the prospect of a chat and said, "Good evening to you, boy."

"Good evening."

He was a tall man, middle-aged, with bushy, sand-colored hair and eyebrows. Perhaps he had been red-haired once. He had a slow way with him, in speech as well as in movement, which as I later found gave him time to think before he spoke. His eyes were light-blue, very sharp and penetrating. He pointed with the stem of his pipe at my bundle.

"You have a tent there. Are you looking for a place to camp?"

"Yes," I said. "A sheltered place, not too near the sea. Do you own the wood across the road?"

"I wish I did," he said. "But you can go in there if you like and no one will say a word to you. The people that own it only come for the summer and there's no sign of them yet. It's a disgrace to have that house and land idle for ten months of the year."

I had never thought in this way before, since it had always been said to me that a man can do as he pleases with his own property. It was different in Connemara, as I soon found out.

"I'll only stay there one night," I said. "I want to go farther west."

"Walking?"

"Yes."

He gave a short laugh. " 'Tis fine exercise, if you don't have to walk all day in the way of business. I'll come with you and give a hand with the tent."

He came out onto the road and showed me where a neatly built stile of stone led into the wood. The land dropped away a little here, so that the wall gave excellent shelter. He helped me to erect my tent so expertly that I said, "It's not the first time you did that."

"No," he said. "I was in the army for a while, and they teach you all kinds of things there—some useful and some not. Ned

Hernon is my name, and I have a son John, about the same age as yourself. He's out after sheep this evening but he'll be home later on, and I'm thinking he'd like to see this little house of yours. So if you have a visitor, you needn't be surprised."

Then I had to tell him my name, and that I had never been in Connemara before and had no relations there, and that my mother said fresh air was good for a city boy, and that I was not afraid to sleep outside alone. When he had left me, I got out my little stove and began to cook my supper.

## 3

BREAD AND BUTTER AND sausages make a fine meal. The sausages were quickly cooked, and the sight of them gave me such a feeling of benevolence that I handed a crumb of one to a passing beetle that was hurrying through the short grass. It was a wonderful feast, and it had the effect of making my encampment feel quite homelike. The aroma of the sausages was the chief cause of this, I think.

When I had finished, I washed up in the stream a few yards away. Then I laid out my sleeping bag in the tent. Night was still a long way off, but it seemed that the trees had moved a little nearer. They were short, and grew closely together as if they were huddled against the wind. Their top branches were all intertwined so that they formed a sort of roof that sloped away from the sea. Though it was only the beginning of summer, already the edges of the trees were curled and brown from the salt wind, so that they had a look of autumn. Hundreds of jackdaws had their nests up there, and the air was full of their high, sharp voices.

Then, without a sound, all at once a red-haired boy was standing on top of the wall by the stile. His eyes rested on my tent with delight, as I could see. He leaped to the ground, as light as a fox, and came across to where I stood.

"Isn't it well for you?" he said at once. "What I wouldn't give for a little tent like that! Things are too quiet. When my grandfather was young, they had great times, out fighting the Black and Tans, sleeping in sheds and under haystacks, telling stories, singing songs." He stopped suddenly, and then added, "That's if it's true for them. My name is John Hernon. It was my father that helped you to put up the tent."

"Come inside and have a look at it," I said.

He crawled inside, and I squatted in the entry, watching him. Then I said, "It seems to me that people make their own fun. And maybe you could have more fun without a war going on all around you. I like it quiet, myself."

"I don't," he said eagerly. "They all look so wild and lively when they get talking about the old times. I suppose they've forgotten about the bullets." He paused to think about this, and then said, "I'm going fishing for sharks tomorrow."

"That doesn't sound such a quiet life."

"They're easy old things. Would you like to come?"

"How do you go about it?" I asked cautiously.

"We go out in the currachs. We have harpoons. You'll see it all if you come with us."

I could not refuse this invitation without losing my new reputation for courage and independence. I had never heard that sharks were easy old things, to be dismissed with a shrug of contempt. In fact I had read various accounts of their persistence in following boats in the Atlantic Ocean, in the hope that someone would fall out, or at least trail an arm or a leg over the side so that it could be bitten off.

"Do you often go shark fishing?"

"Every summer. It's great sport. They come floating in on the top of the water, taking the sun. They like it warm, and they stay in the Gulf Stream until it strikes the coast of Ireland."

"What do you want them for?"

"For the liver, man. You should see it—as big as a kitchen table. The rest of the shark is no good, though I've heard they eat whales in some parts of the world. I wouldn't fancy that myself. The day they'd be having whale, I'd ask for a boiled egg, so I would."

"Maybe you wouldn't if you were brought up to it," I suggested.

"Maybe. So I'll be down for you at seven o'clock in the morning. It's no good going out too early because the sharks won't come in until the sun is warm and the tide flowing. You're used to boats, I suppose."

"Yes," I said, and was glad he asked no more about that. My experience was all on the lake at home, Lough Allen, that I once thought must be the biggest sheet of water in the world. By comparison with Galway Bay, it was no bigger than one of the fields I had passed by the roadside. I added, "But I'm not used to sharks."

"You will be—after tomorrow," he said.

Then he invited me to cross the road with him and make the acquaintance of the rest of the family. I was glad to do this, because while he had been talking the woods had darkened still further and I had not liked the prospect of sitting in my tent alone while the night closed blackly in around me.

The Hernons' kitchen was full of people, it seemed to me. Supper was over and the floor had been swept and the fire made up. The evening had got rather cold when darkness fell, and a big semi-circle of chairs was arranged in such a way that everyone could enjoy a share of the fire's warmth.

Ned Hernon had a big chair at the side of the fire farthest from the door, so that he could see anyone who came in or out. Opposite him, on the hob, sat a lively little old man who I guessed was his father, the hero of the stories that had made his grandson so envious. On the other hob, a pleasant-faced woman sat knitting a white sweater. It was a complicated pattern and she hardly lifted her eyes from it all evening except when I came in with John, and later when she and her daughter made tea for us all. The rest of the company consisted of John's two older brothers, Pat and Tim, and his sister Mary.

The brothers were grown men to my eye, tough and weather-beaten. Mary looked to be just a little older than John. She was very like her mother, with fair curly hair and a humorous expression. As soon as I had been given a chair in the circle, she went on with what she had been saying:

"I wouldn't go shark fishing for the whole wide world. Such ugly faces they have!"

"We don't hunt them for their beauty," said Pat.

"And afterward you leave them on the shore, and no one can go down there for weeks with the smell they make," she said.

"Only until the seagulls clear it away," said Tim. "They're mighty thankful to us. And the liver—"

"Don't talk to me about the liver!" She covered her face with both her hands. They laughed good-humoredly.

The old man said, " 'Tis great sport hunting sharks, but when they get cross, they're dangerous old devils. I remember once we went out—it would be nearly forty years ago now, I suppose—myself and Michael Rohan and a man from Letter-more. We were off Rossaveel, about halfway across the Bay, when we saw your man sailing along with the fin up. We landed the harpoon on him, but instead of making off for the wide ocean, didn't he go for the boat. I thought my last hour had come. Said I to myself, a man should make his peace with God before he goes out after this kind of sport, for you never know how the day will end."

"What happened?" I asked, eagerly enough you may be sure.

"The harpoon had weakened him and he couldn't upset the boat, but he tried his best, so he did. He was the cleverest shark I ever met in these parts. Mostly they have no sense at all."

"I heard of that happening to another man," said Ned, "but it never happened to me. I think the sharks that come here are tired, they're so far from home. There's never much fight in them."

Strangely enough, instead of frightening me off, this talk

had the effect of making me eager for the next day's sport. The biggest fish I had ever seen was a twenty-two-pound salmon, and the man that had caught him had had all he could do to get him landed. The notion of landing a fish whose liver would be the size of a kitchen table was beyond imagining. I could hardly wait until the next day to see how it would be done.

A high, clear moon gave me light enough to find my way back to my camp at last. It would have been enough to light up my tent too, but I lit a candle for company and because I preferred its warm yellow light to the pale light of the moon.

As I lay in my sleeping bag, it occurred to me that I had not heard nor asked for any news of Michael Joyce's deer. I put the thought away from me, feeling a delightful drowsiness creep over my whole body. Tomorrow I would begin on all that. Just now the most important thing was to go to sleep before the secret people of the woods would begin their night's business. Fortunately I was so tired that there was time only for the vaguest thought of pookas and banshees before I was fast asleep.

The heat of the sun woke me long before John came to fetch me at seven o'clock. The dark-green canvas of the tent was hot to touch. Before I moved out of my sleeping bag, I looked up and saw how dozens of flies had come in during the night, out of the cold I suppose, and were congregated in the warmest places where the sun's rays struck directly. A tent is like a greenhouse, I discovered that morning, and there is nothing to be done but get up and out of it early.

I made breakfast of a cold sausage with bread and butter, and water from the spring at the head of the stream. Then I rolled up my sleeping bag, swished the flies outside, and tied the flap of the tent close. I was sitting on top of the wall waiting when John came out of his own front door.

He made me take off my boots and leave them in his kitchen. Then we were on our way to the sea. The others had already gone, he said. In case we might be out late, he had brought a few crusts of bread. I asked, "Don't they mind bringing me with them?"

"No, indeed. The heavier the boat is, the better they like it. You'll see."

To reach the sea we had to cross three little fields, hopping over the loose stone walls wherever they were low enough. Then we came to a long curved beach that sloped sharply down to the sea. Most of it was covered with heavy white stones, worn smooth and round by the sea, so that they looked like a fantastic collection of huge birds' eggs. Walking on them was a painful business, as they had a way of rolling slowly but powerfully onto the bare toes.

The sea was quite smooth, so pale as to be almost gray, and shining in the sunlight. The Clare mountains across the bay were a stronger blue. A little off the shore there was a tiny, bare island, and already at this hour we could see a man out there cutting seaweed from its rocky sides and loading it into his currach. The weed was piled high in the boat, so that it was sunk to its gunwales.

"That's Andy Cooney," said John, seeing me looking out at the island. "He must be the first man out of bed in the whole world. The low tide was at five o'clock and by the look of things he has been out there since that hour, if not earlier. He'll have that weed carted home and stacked before dinner, if I know him. And no one to help him but the dog."

Near us, at the edge of the sea, the Hernons' currach was already afloat. I was surprised to see Ned's father there. As soon as we came up, he looked at me with a humorous eye and said, "You're wondering is that old fellow going out in the boat after sharks."

"I thought you said you don't go any more," I mumbled, embarrassed at having my feelings read so clearly.

"And I don't," he said, "but I'm able to give a shove off to the currach still, and to see that everything is shipshape."

The currach was a shock to me, but I tried to conceal my

feelings since I had been warned how they showed. Silently and with as blank an expression as I could manage, I examined it closely. I had never seen a boat like it before. On the lake at home, we had heavy wooden boats, businesslike and slow. If one owned land on one of the islands, bales of hay or sacks of potatoes, and even sheep and young cattle could be brought to or from it in those boats. The heavy creaking timbers and the long, broad-bladed oars gave one a feeling of safety, though if a storm came up suddenly, I had often heard, the whole craft might turn over.

The currach was a light framework of wood with canvas stretched over it. The canvas was tarred, and I saw a patch or two which had been put on to cover small tears in it. The bows were sharp and curved rather strangely upward, and the stern was square and low. The currach seemed as light as a feather. It drew only an inch or two of water, and it was moored by a thin rope to a stone which would not have held one of our boats for five minutes. There were two pairs of oars, with no blades at all that I could see, though they were cut flatter at the end where the blades should have been.

The men had just finished going over their gear when we arrived. They had two coils of strong rope, not very thick but closely spun. They had a harpoon gun which looked as if it had seen a hundred years' service. The rest of their equipment consisted of a couple of billhooks. Ned and his two elder sons were wearing sea-boots and fine, heavy, knitted sweaters. John and I were in our bare feet. He had brought a heavy sweater for me, having guessed that I would not have one warm enough.

Ned said, "Peter, since you have never been in a currach before, I suppose, you'd best go in the stern."

I made to board the currach, but found out that there was a special skill in this. First she was cast off, and the grandfather held her by the gunwale. Then we all waded into the water. When she was well afloat, first John and then I climbed aboard and sat low and quiet at either end. Then the three men in their sea-boots walked in up to their knees, pushing the boat with them, and all at once leaped aboard so that we rocked and danced about on the water. Instantly Ned and Pat had a pair of oars each and were rowing as if the hounds of hell were after them. We flew over the water, and I saw that those slim little oars were well able for their business. I supposed that it was force of habit that had made the men so fierce about it. With this calm sea it had been easy enough, but I could imagine what speed and good timing would be needed to get a currach afloat if the waves were rolling in.

By the time I had the courage to turn my head and look back, we were half a mile out to sea. On the shore, I could see the tiny figure of the grandfather clambering over the rocks on his way home. The greenness of the land astonished me. From out here, all the colors seemed sharpened. The houses showed glittering, as if they had been whitewashed that very morning. On the low hills inland, the furze shone like polished gold. Beyond that, the mountains were a clear, strong blue.

"It will be a grand day," said Ned, "with the mountains that color. This is the weather to bring in the sharks."

"Where will you find them?"

Galway Bay looked too big to be scoured for sharks in a boat the size of a currach.

"Not too far offshore," said Ned. "I suppose the farther out you go, the colder the water gets, and those lads like to be comfortable. They come in around Aran a lot. The Aranmen are always watching out for them, but they can't stop a few of them from coming along to us."

Now there was a gentle swell, and we rolled smoothly up and over it. The water tickled the thin canvas of the currach. Since I had become accustomed to its motion, I was no longer frightened. My low position gave me a feeling of security, as I could not look down into the depths of the sea without leaning over the side, and I guessed that this would not have been allowed.

I think I had hardly believed that the sharks would keep their appointment with us until I heard John call out, "Here they come! Two of the devils!"

Instantly the men stopped rowing, holding their oars high so that the water ran off them in a chain of glittering drops. Everyone was following John's pointing finger. It was well that no one was looking at me. Though I stayed as still as a stone, I could feel my heart pounding like a blacksmith's hammer inside my sweater, and I am sure it was a minute before I was able to look with some measure of calm in the direction of the sharks.

When I had spotted them, my first feeling was one of great relief. All that showed was a pair of black, triangular fins, like

tiny sails, moving rather slowly along. Occasionally one or the other of them would disappear for a few seconds while the shark rolled over to enjoy the sun on its belly. Then it would come into view again, always keeping pace with its companion. One fin was twice the size of the other.

The men were rowing vigorously again.

"A big one and a small one," said Ned, and his voice was thick with excitement. "We can go for the big one. There's enough of us. The currach is well weighted. Tim, have you the harpoon ready?"

It was ready in his hand, though the sharks were still hundreds of yards away. Lazily they rolled over, and I saw a gleam of white skin in the strong sunlight. As we came closer, I noticed that the men used a different stroke of the oars, shorter and cutting the water almost at right angles, so as to make little splash. The sharks paid no attention, continuing as if they were on their way quietly to Galway. It was extraordinary to see how Ned and his son were able to work perfectly together without exchanging a single word. Perhaps Ned's move came a second before Pat's but the gap was so small as to be hardly distinguishable.

Now they turned the currach so that its bows were facing west, toward the mouth of the bay. From where we were, the Aran Islands looked nearer, and I found myself curious about the people who lived there. It certainly seemed likely that they had more excitement every day than we in our village in Leitrim would see in a month.

The motion of the currach had changed, and the men were maneuvering it broadside onto the track of the sharks. I had seen angry horses sidle toward each other in this way. The sharks rolled on unconcerned, prepared, it seemed, to pass within a few feet of us.

Then I saw the harpoon fly through the air, with its rope sailing after it. All movement stopped in the currach, so that you would think everyone had suddenly died. With a queer hissing sound, the harpoon cut through the water, and then a tremendous shower of spray went up as the shark leaped out of the water.

"Got him, the old devil!"

"Hold, hold!"

"Watch him!"

"Watch when he starts going!"

They were all shouting instructions to each other. There seemed to be little need for it as each seemed alert and ready to do things he had done with precision a hundred times before.

No one was watching me. What idea was in my head I don't know to this day. Perhaps there was none. All I know is that I took one of the billhooks and tied the end of the second coil of rope to its handle, in the narrowest part of the grip. It was wonderful rope, thin and closely woven, and it made a tight, powerful knot.

The big shark rolled and turned and splashed, and thrashed the water with its furious tail. Tim held the rope, letting it go slack. Pat and Ned sat half-turned on the thwarts, holding their oars high. Suddenly they shipped them. The rope of the harpoon tightened. Now all three of them grasped it, while the shark began to swim out for the open sea. I saw John in the bows quickly tie the end of the rope in a hard knot to the framework of the gunwale. The thought flashed through my mind that if the shark were to give a sudden jerk, it could wrench a piece of the gunwale away. If it were to dive— But it did neither of these things. Its movement was smooth, though if we had not been five in the currach we would have been towed too fast for safety. As it was, our speed was less than when the men had been rowing their hardest.

Then I did an extraordinary thing, quite as surprising to myself as it was to everyone else. Instead of following its companion, the smaller shark had submerged and was circling the currach, quite close. Everyone was busy with the harpoon rope. I poked my head up to see the small shark pass by at one side of us, roll over as it crossed the stern, and come by the other side almost on its back, with its great ugly mouth showing in a kind of snarl. I could not resist the impulse that seized me. Perhaps I was remembering the grandfather's story of the shark that attacked the currach. Whatever the reason, I took the billhook with both hands, leaned over the side, and plunged the blade as deeply as I could into the shark's body.

A shudder seemed to go through the currach. My shark was whacking the water with its tail. I let out some of the rope to give it room. You may be sure the rest of the party was looking at me now. Ned gave a shout of laughter. I must have looked ridiculous, with all my terror showing on my face. Ned slid to his knees and leaned forward to help with the rope, which was already moving painfully through my fingers.

"I don't know will we hold him," he said in an almost confi-

dential tone. "That's not a fishhook you have there." He laughed again with delight. "Maybe I'll lose my old billhook. Fishing sharks with a billhook is a new sport."

His eyes danced with amusement. This was going to be a story to tell for the rest of his life. There was no time to wonder how I would figure in it.

It was obvious that we could not afford to tie the end of the rope to the frame of the currach as I had seen John do, since it was not yet certain which direction our shark would take. If it had chosen to go in a different direction from its companion, we should have had to turn it loose. Fortunately, however, it followed the bigger shark, as I suppose it had done for thousands of miles. Gradually Ned paid out more and more rope, while our shark seemed to hurry forward to join the other. For an extraordinary spell of time, which seemed a lifetime to me, we were towed along by our pair of sea monsters, like a boatful of enchanted heroes in one of the ancient Irish stories.

Then gradually we were going more slowly, and I felt that I could not bear to watch what was happening any more. A flock of seagulls had gathered shrieking above us, attracted by the sharks' blood. I closed my eyes and sat back in the stern as low as I could. I had often gone for a day's fishing at home, but there had been some sense to the size of the fish we caught.

However, there was no getting out of finishing what I had begun. John and Tim together had to attend to the big shark, and their father took charge of the small one, which he hauled in until it trailed, floating, close behind us. That left only Pat to row the currach, unless I were to take a hand. There was nothing for it but to crawl onto the thwart and take Ned's oars. Very slowly, we turned the currach's bows toward the shore, while John and Tim maneuvered their shark, on the end of its rope, so that it trailed astern with the other.

I gave all my attention to my oars. They were easier to use than the broad-bladed ones to which I was accustomed. They were lighter, and they sat firmly on a strong, tall peg instead of fitting into a metal oarlock.

With our heavy load, we could make little headway. The tide had turned and a little wind had sprung up as well, so that the journey back took an age. The oars which had seemed so light at first, after half an hour were like to pull my arms out of their sockets. I dared not show how tired I was. None of the others gave any sign of fatigue. In fact they chatted among themselves about the easy day that this had been, and how they had often rowed twice as far and brought home nothing but a few mackerel.

"And this time we have two sharks," said Ned several times, as if he enjoyed counting them. "Wait till my father sees them —*he'll* be a picture to see. *Two* sharks! And one of them speared on a billhook, as neat as you please."

They had some talk that I tried not to hear, about why the billhook had not come out, nor cut through the shark. It seemed that I had struck it exactly in the right spot, as if I were an expert in the anatomy of sharks.

Ned had his eyes fixed on the shore. At long last he said, "They have us spotted. There's a currach coming out. I don't know yet who is in it—Tomeen Cooney, I think, and maybe Morgan Curran. Wait till they see what we have!"

We had not long to wait. In a few minutes they were circling around us, admiring and wondering at our catch. Then they shot back to the shore, making their currach fly in their anxiety to get the story told to the little group that was waiting there. As we came closer in I could hear exclamations.

"*Two* sharks!"

"Two of them!"

"The like was never heard of before."

"We'll be the talk of the world."

"*Two* sharks!"

"This news should be in all the papers of the world."

And then, all at once, I was a hero. I was handed ashore like the Queen of Sheba. A circle of admirers gathered around me. I felt like Jack the Giant Killer as Ned explained how I had stabbed the second shark in the moment before it would have got away. Everyone shook my hand. The grandfather was especially delighted. A boy like me, he said, would make his fortune in no time. Such intelligence, such resourcefulness!

At last they let me go, hot all over with embarrassment at all this admiration. It was true, after all, that basking sharks were easy old things. My heroism had consisted only in striking one instinctive blow, which ordinary common sense should have told me not to do.

When the sharks were beached, with the help of all the neighbors, we had a long look at them. The big shark was a good size, they said, about twelve feet from its ugly snout to its big, strong tail. Mine was about half that length. The jaws looked wicked enough to bite a man in two, but everyone agreed that it was almost unknown for them to attack. A conger eel was a lot worse, they said. One of those lads would bite the hand off you if he got the chance.

"Keep well away from those," they advised me solemnly, "until we give you a few lessons in how to catch them."

It was taken for granted that with my kind of luck and skill, I would naturally take up monster fishing for a living. And I soon found out that the liver of the smaller shark was my property. They would all show me how to take it out and cut it up, and how to put it in a barrel until the oil ran out. Hoping that the very thought of this process had not turned my face green, I said to Ned, "I'd be glad if you would take it. I did nothing to earn it except stick your billhook into it, and you said yourself that I might have lost that."

"It was well worth the chance," he said eagerly.

"And it was your boat and your rope," I said firmly, "and indeed I'll be very glad if you'll take that shark for your own."

So he agreed, and we left the two huge fish well above the high-water line and marched off home.

The grandfather was out in front, almost dancing with excitement. Then, rather sadly, he said, "God be with the days when I'd have been out there myself. The sport we had! I remember one fish that brought us away out beyond Aran, and the Aranmen came out and said he was theirs because he was in their waters, and it nearly came to a fight. But we kept the fish and we came home by moonlight that night, I remember well, though we had been out since dawn, and we singing all the way."

So we had been fortunate, it seemed, in getting our sharks quickly and so reaching home for dinner time. I doubt if we would have come back before nightfall, without one. I envied the men their toughness, especially John, who was as well able for this wild, rough life as any of the older men. I thought of the few little crusts of bread, which seemed to be all the food he had brought. He had not even thought of taking them out to nibble. The salt air had made me so hungry that my legs would hardly carry me. I walked into the Hernons' kitchen in a sort of dream and noticed at once that a big, round, hanging pot was boiling over the fire, and another, flatter one was sizzling on the hearth. A great smell of dinner was floating about, and the knives and forks were already on the table.

At once the story of the two sharks had to be told again, but neither Mary nor her mother slowed their preparations for dinner by so much as a second while they listened. Tim was given the potato pot to strain, as if he had been idle all morning. Then suddenly Mary said, "That's enough about those sharks. If I hear one word about them while we're eating our dinner, the whole lot of you will go hungry tonight."

They looked startled, but after a moment Ned said, "The girl is right. There's a time to talk about sharks and a time to keep quiet about them. And there's men's talk and women's talk. While we're eating our dinner, you can tell us what you were doing here at home while we were on the sea."

# ✺ 4

A CHAIR WAS BROUGHT to the table for me too, as if I were one of the family. Indeed I felt as if I had known these people all my life—they were so friendly and natural. They must have felt the same toward me, because in the talk that followed no one gave any sign of doubt about the safety of letting me hear what they were saying.

We were no sooner started on dinner than the old man gave a hoot of laughter, holding his potato judicially in the air as he peeled it.

"You've had a great morning," he said. "You think no one else had a bit of excitement but yourselves. Patsy Carroll was here."

"Looking for me?" Ned asked.

"Yes. About the deer. He wants to know what he's to do next."

"Are they sick?"

"No, faith. He says they're in great fettle."

"Good."

"But he says Colman Donnelly is getting frightened, and says he won't keep them in his place any more. He said if the Guards come out from Galway, the first place they'll search will be his. Mind you, Patsy was inclined to agree with him. It wouldn't be the first time that a man sold his land and got sorry after, and took revenge, as you might say, on the man that bought it."

"Colman is only half a man," said Ned with contempt. "But maybe he's right this time," he added after a moment. "I suppose we'd better move them."

"There's an easier way than that," said the old man softly.

"What is it?"

"You could slaughter them. There's great eating on a deer. That's what we did in the old times, as you know well, when my lord put deer on the island and thought they died out because the air didn't suit them. God help his head! If he had a right look at the bones, he would have seen that there was a lot missing. I was good at butchering a deer in my day. I'll show you—"

Mary slapped the table with her hand suddenly and said, "No talk of deer or sharks, I'm warning you."

"All right, all right," said the old man. "But you'll cook the meat fine, if I bring it home."

"It would be a change from bacon and old roosters," she said.

Ned was looking worried. "I don't like that way. As long as they're alive, we can always back out—"

"Back out! Why would you back out? And leave six hundred and odd acres of land to fill the bellies of those useless animals! You must fight, man! Fight for the right to use the sacred soil of Ireland to rear children, and decent animals like cows and pigs, that a person could have a bit of respect for. We fought long and hard for our rights—the days are gone when a landlord could clear the tenants off to America and make a deer park to show off to his visitors."

"Mr. Joyce didn't clear off any tenants," said Ned. "That fight is long over and won. This is a different thing. And I'm not changing my mind. All I want is what everyone wants—to see the land being used in some decent way, or else to have it divided out among them that could use it."

I kept my eyes on my dinner while this was going on. I had learned so many things in the last few minutes that I should have been feeling very pleased with myself. Instead, I found myself longing to tell everyone there that I was a spy, and that all their kindness to me would only be repaid by my revealing their secrets. It was a very unpleasant sensation, and one that I should have anticipated before I got myself into this situation. I have often heard since that time that spies enjoy a feeling of power because they know so much about everyone's business. All I can say is that I felt nothing of the sort, only that I had got into a mean trade for the sake of money. However, I did not say anything now. After all, I had not yet passed on anything that I had learned, and there would be time enough later to think over the morality of the question.

Ned was saying, "Driving off the deer and hiding them is a fairly harmless thing to do. We can put them back if we want to. Killing them would be barefaced robbery and we'd have the Guards after us—"

The old man interrupted him with a derisive hoot. "When I was young, we weren't afraid of no Guards!"

"Times have changed, Father," said Ned patiently. "And in your day there were no Guards, only the Royal Irish Constabulary, the king's men. And you agreed that we should try this way first."

"I did, sure," said his father. "I must be getting old, I suppose. There was a time when I wasn't so quiet. There was a time when I wouldn't have thought only of slaughtering deer." He finished his dinner silently and went outside to brood about it, I suppose.

Ned said to his wife, "Is Patsy Carroll going to come back?"

"No. But he said for you to go to his place after dinner, because you must make a few plans. And remember you promised there would be no slaughtering of those deer. There's no need for it. Your father would like to bring back the old times, I'm thinking. If he got a few old fighting lads like himself, they might do harm before anyone could stop them."

"I doubt if he'd find anyone to help him. He couldn't do it alone."

"You'd never know," said Mrs. Hernon. "Sometimes there of an afternoon, I do be sitting on the hob getting on with a bit of sewing or knitting, and your father would be opposite me, and in comes Jock Feeney or Roddy Faherty or Matteen the Tailor, and in two shakes of a lamb's tail they're fighting the Black and Tans and the Royal Irish Constabulary all over again, until they have rivers of blood flowing through my kitchen. If they see me smiling, they get mad and they all set on me together as if I were a traitor of the deepest dye. I always have to give your father a drop out of the bottle when they're gone, to quiet him down."

" 'Tis true, they excite each other," said Ned, "but I think it's all talk. If you think they're planning any action, you can give me a warning and I'll be talking to them."

After dinner, I was in two minds about what to do. On the one hand, I was tempted to move on at once and see for myself what sort of place Michael Joyce lived in, and perhaps judge whether his land was worth all the trouble it was causing. I knew enough now to be able to make a good start on explaining to him why his deer had been stolen. On the other hand, by staying here one night longer I might learn what was going to happen now.

In the end, it was John that decided I would stay. When he realized that I was considering striking my tent and moving on, he said, "And what in the world would make you do that? Aren't you as free as air? You can go where you like, sleep where you like, stay as long as you like in any place that takes you fancy."

"That's true."

"And even if you want to see the whole of Connemara, haven't you the summer before you? I must go out now in a small while and lay a string of lobster pots. Let you come with me, and we'll come back here afterward and have our supper, and have the evening long for talking."

I could not possibly have refused. John took an old canvas sack and a long, wicked-looking knife from the shed at the end of the house. Then he led the way down to the strand again, this time whistling to his sheep dog to come along too. These Connemara dogs astonished me. They seemed to have no prejudices at all against going in boats. Our dogs never came with us on the lake—they would come as far as the shore and then run up and down barking anxiously until we were out of earshot, as if they were warning us of the danger we were in. John's dog seemed to take it for granted that he would come with us, as I had seen Andy Cooney's dog do earlier that morning on the island.

The seagulls were circling, screaming, around the sharks when we reached the strand. They kept a distance, though, and John said it was because they were not yet quite sure if the sharks were dead.

"Shark meat makes fine bait for the lobsters," he said, and in two shakes he had hacked off a great slice and put it in his bag.

We took the currach from the top of the strand, where the men had left it, and John showed me how to turn it upside down and get underneath it, so that we carried it down to the sea's edge on our shoulders.

On the hard sand we turned the currach right side up again, and went back for the oars.

"The lobster pots are at the quay," John said. "I see we have a couple of helpers."

Sure enough, two men were lounging there, smoking their pipes in the sunny afternoon. We pushed off and took a pair of oars each. The tide was almost at its lowest ebb, and a reef of rocks now showed parallel with the quay. We rounded its tip and pulled in to the steps. The quay wall towered above us, and in its shadow the water of the tiny harbor looked inky black. John reached up and moored the currach to an iron ring set in the wall. Then we skipped up the slippery steps in our bare feet to get the lobster pots. The dog followed so easily that I could see he had done it many times before.

The pots were stacked on the quay waiting for us. They looked like wicker-work cages, I thought. Each one had a funnel-shaped entry at one end, through which the lobsters could pass. Once inside, John said, they could not come out again as they had not the wits for it. This seemed very strange to me but I found out later that it was quite true.

The two men who had been leaning on the wall came slowly over to us. One of them said at once, "Well, did you get the hero's portion for dinner?"

Then I recognized them as the two men who had come out in the currach to see our catch that morning.

"I have the hero's portion here in the bag, Morgan," said John, taking out the slice of shark meat. "Let ye help us now to bait the pots with it."

"Ah, sure, the lobsters will get it after all," Morgan said. As he and his companion took out their knives and began to cut up the meat for bait, he said, "You can leave me the little bit of skin, for rubbing down the new chair I'm making."

John presented him solemnly with the skin, which was rough like sandpaper. Afterward he told me that he had been hard put to it not to laugh outright. Morgan always saved everything useful, however small, and he often annoyed people by asking for something they had intended to keep for themselves. The new chair had been made from pieces of timber begged here and there from people making boats or building extensions to their houses. Not having to buy so much as a piece of sandpaper to smooth it with must have been a great satisfaction to Morgan, John said.

Each pot had a fair-sized stone inside, to sink it. We tied a piece of shark meat to each stone by a short length of string. Then one by one we carried the pots down the steps and stacked them high in the stern of the currach. The pots were

strung together on a long rope, ending with some flat corks
which would act as floats to show the exact position of the
string.

Slowly and calmly the baiting and loading was done, and
slowly and unhurriedly we shoved off again from the quay with
our load. By the tip of the reef we dropped the pots overboard,
one by one, and watched them sink. Then we rowed back to
the strand, beached the currach, and carried it up to the top of
the strand, where we placed heavy stones against it so that it
would not blow away if a wind came up.

The whole afternoon was gone. On the warm sand, the dog
stretched himself with his paws pushed out long in front of him
and his slim pink tongue quivering outside his open jaws.

"Look at him," said John. "You'd think he had done a day's
work, to be so tired. It's a funny thing that after a day on the
mountain after sheep, when he should be really tired from
working, he springs around at this time of the evening quite
lively. It looks as if work suits him better than idleness."

When we reached the Hernons' house, Ned had not yet re-
turned. We paid a visit to my camp to make sure that everything was in order. As I had noticed already, one night spent
there had made it feel like home. I knew that all my life long
the memory of the field would remain in my mind, as would
that of any other place where I would put up my tent. It was as

if even in one night I had somehow grown roots that attached me to it.

Supper was just starting in Hernons' when Ned came in. It was a feast for a king. There was a mountain of soda-bread, still warm from the pot-oven. There were two dishes of salty, homemade butter, each with a cow's head imprinted on it and each in a special glass dish shaped like a hen sitting on a nest. There was a whole clutch of hard-boiled eggs so that anyone who liked could have two or three. There was a dish of blackberry jam, and in case anyone might still be hungry, just at the end Mary brought over a plate of currant bread to finish up with. We washed it all down with cups of tea out of a huge brown teapot.

When she was sure that everyone had had enough, Mrs. Hernon said, "Pull over to the fire now, and we'll hear the news."

"The shark meat was handy for baiting the lobster pots," said John, and he gave an account of our work.

Pat and Tim had finished mowing a hayfield. "We found two honeycombs," said Pat, "one each. The bees were hopping mad. But sure they have the whole summer long to make more."

"Maybe they'll have lost their courage with those ones," said Mary.

"You saw Patsy Carroll?" said the old man to Ned.

While we had been eating, he had looked imploringly at Mrs. Hernon many times, but she pretended to take no notice. This confirmed what I had guessed, that the women of this household had made some kind of a rule that no subject which might lead to an argument or any kind of unpleasantness was to be discussed during meals. It must have been good for the digestions of the whole family. It seemed an excellent idea to me. One of the things I most disliked about my cousin, the sheep farmer, was that he saw meal times as a golden opportunity for discussing every controversial subject one could imagine, from my high notions to my mother's failure to get the top price for her young cattle.

"Yes, I saw Patsy," said Ned. "We're moving the deer. He's going about it tonight."

I felt myself get the fidgets immediately. I had to sit still, though it seemed to me that I should be out on the road to Michael Joyce's place at once, to warn him that his deer were going to go even farther away. This thought proved that I really was working for Michael Joyce and made me still more uncomfortable.

Ned was saying, "Morgan is going with Patsy. They'll take the horses. It's the quietest way."

"Where will they take them?"

"To Inish Goill, maybe, if they can manage them easy. It's not like driving sheep. And it's a long road."

"A good place, though," said the old man eagerly. "Well worth the trouble."

"Patsy will be down some night to tell me how they fared," said Ned. "He'll do it fine. There's nothing Patsy puts his hand to that he doesn't do well."

Then they talked of other things, mostly about the sharks and the lobsters, and the great start that had been made to the summer with our catch today. The weather was settled, they said, and would be good for all kinds of fishing. And they recalled the shoal of mackerel that had come in at this time last year, so plentiful that you could catch them in a basket below at the quay. I found out that for the next month or two their time would be taken up with fishing. When they would have the hay saved, there was little farming to do except to look after the livestock, since no one grew much corn. They would cut turf too, they said, and dry it for the winter's fires. Still, I could see that in the long summer evenings there would be plenty of time for chat and talk, and for planning how best to discourage Michael Joyce from his peculiar farming habits.

So far as I could see, it was the *oddity* of keeping deer that they resented most. Close after that, as I had suspected from the first, came the dislike of seeing one person with such a big farm of land, even if he had bought and paid for it, while others had so little. This could be called envy, plain and simple, but I knew that in Ireland it went deeper. The land itself was counted a holy thing, to be respected and prized. The former owner, Colman Donnelly, had been a bad farmer, and had probably left the land idle. I wondered if his father had been any better, but of course there was no question of asking. By chance I might reveal that I knew more than I had pretended, since I had not yet sorted out the different sources of my information.

At last I went back to sleep in my tent. John accompanied me, carrying a lantern, and waited, watching with interest, until I was in my sleeping bag. Then he went off home and I was left in utter darkness. All the same, that night I found that I was not so nervous. The sea air was like a drug, and I had had plenty of it, both morning and afternoon. Soon I dropped into a heavy sleep, and did not wake until the jackdaws called me in the morning.

After a breakfast of porridge, I began to strike camp. There was a nip in the air this morning that had not been there yesterday. Still, the sky was clear of clouds and the sun was shining down into my little field. I made a neat, tight pack of my belongings and hoisted them onto my back. Then I climbed the stile and crossed the road to say good-by to the Hernon family.

Though it was hardly eight o'clock, Ned had already gone out. They were cutting up the sharks today, John explained, before the seagulls would have polished them off and before they would have begun to rot. Ned had gone over to the village to investigate a rumour that the entire carcass of a shark could be sold now, and not merely the liver as had been the case formerly. A man from Galway would come out with a lorry and take them away. They would be converted into fishmeal which could be used either as an animal food or as top dressing on the land.

"You may be sure we'll be thankful to that man if the story is true," said Mrs. Hernon. "No one wants to eat a shark, God knows, and still it goes through me to see that big body feeding the seagulls that are well able to do their own fishing. And worst of all is that the whole summer long the bones lie on the strand unless the sea washes them away. And the stench is around there so that a person can't take a walk on the shore for a month."

"They say that they grind up the bones too," John said. "I'd never have thought fish bones could be eaten, even by animals."

The grandfather had gone directly to the shore with old Jock Feeney, who had worked on a whaling ship and knew all about how to extract a shark's liver. It would be an interesting morning, John said, but I was not at all tempted to stay. Promising to come in again on my way home, if I passed this way, I left them at last and started off toward the west.

After half a mile or so I came to the village of Salleen. It was a fine big village with a wide main street, several shops, and the church with the spire that I had seen in the distance. Though it was so early, everyone seemed to be stirring. All the doors stood open to let in the sunny air, and as I passed by one of the shops, Ned Hernon came to the door and called out to me, "Safe journey to you! Come back soon!"

Then I was out of the village. I passed by a stunted wood with a little river flowing through it, and at the sea side a road that led down to the quay where we had baited the lobster pots. After that it was all wild, windy country with no shelter anywhere, though the road had curved inland from the sea. Low stone walls wriggled up and over the hills, dividing the land into rocky fields. The little thatched houses were bright with whitewash. The air was full of a mixture of the scent of growing grass and turf smoke and of the wallflowers that grew close against the houses, with somewhere in it the strange, strong scent of the sea.

Eight miles is not a long walk and I had no wish to hurry. As I went along, I reviewed my stores of food and realized that I had nothing but a handful of potatoes and a couple of sausages. They would be just enough for a midday meal. Far better to wait until I was at Michael Joyce's village before buying my next supplies. Having business in the shop would perhaps be very useful.

About noon I came to a spring well by the side of the road. I knew it was a good one by the few flat stones that had been laid around it. I filled my little pot with water and opened out my stove and got it alight. Soon four potatoes were bubbling in the water while I lay back at my ease against the sunny wall. When they were cooked, I drained off the water and put them aside while I fried my sausages. It was a good meal, and I congratulated myself on being such a fine cook.

Then, with the taste of the sausages, the thought of the Burkes crossed my mind. Where were they now, I wondered. Perhaps they were on the road to Sligo, crossing the bogs of Mayo. Perhaps they had turned south to Kerry, to join all the tinkers of Ireland at Puck Fair in Killorglin. But it was early for that yet. Puck Fair was not until July. Besides, for some reason the Burkes had had the air of people who would prefer to travel alone. One thing I knew for certain—that it would be a great pleasure to pay them back for the trick they had played on me. I had no idea how this could be done but I hoped that I would recognize the opportunity if it were to offer itself. Well-filled and comfortable with my dinner, I even wondered if it would be possible for me to fight the whole family single-handed.

I moved on again, taking my time. It was no more than five o'clock when I saw a group of houses on either side of the road ahead of me. The road had turned toward the sea again. Some distance farther on, a long grassy hill rose up to a considerable height, sheltering the village from the west wind. At the sea side of the road, after the village, was Michael Joyce's house.

There was no mistaking it—a fine gray, stone house with barns and sheds and coachhouses at one side, and an avenue of trees leading to the door. It was an incongruous sight in that bare landscape, as strange as meeting a zebra or a lion in one's path. The land all around it was better than anything I had seen for miles. This was more proof that it was an old land-lord's house, since those gentry invariably took possession of the best that any district could offer.

With my new experience, as I walked toward it I picked out the perfect place to pitch my tent. It was a field on Michael Joyce's land, close to the hay barn but not too close, with a good stone wall to the sea side. It was such a fine position that I thought it would arouse suspicion if I were not to go there. I need only ask leave, as if I were a stranger to its owner, and after I had made my camp, I could keep well away from the big house.

I walked through the village, therefore, and just beyond it I found a wide iron gate leading into the avenue. What hap-pened then was so unexpected that I let out a little yelp of surprise. As I made to lift the latch of the gate, suddenly a man appeared from behind a tree on the avenue. He was quite close to me and he must have seen me approach. He carried a shot-gun loosely in his right hand, and he crooked his elbow and tightened his grip on the gun in a threatening way as he called out to me, "Take your hand off that gate!"

Anger flowed through me after the first start of surprise. "I was going to ask if I might camp in the field by the barn," I said.

"Well ye can't. There's no campers nor trippers allowed here. Be off with ye!"

His accent was clipped and strange, and the words he used were strange too. What were trippers? I wondered. At first I had thought he said "tinkers," but then the word settled in my mind and I knew that he had used an alien word which had nothing to do with me nor with anyone I knew. Campers were surely few and far between in this windy, remote place, so why should he need to lie in wait with a gun for them?

I was helpless to answer. This must be Michael Joyce's Scotsman, and a poor specimen of humanity he seemed to me.

If there were never a deer in sight, his rough manners would be enough to arouse ill feeling against this household.

As I had never in my life been ordered off in this way, I did not know what to answer. I had dropped my hand from the gate, of course, and now I just turned away without a word and walked back toward the village.

The houses there looked warm and hospitable after the reception I had just had. There was one a little bigger than the rest—a long, thatched house, set back from the road so that a cart could stand in front of it. One was there now, and from the open doorway I could hear the sound of voices.

I crossed the sandy patch and peered into the dimness inside. Several men were there, smoking their pipes in front of the big turf fire. It was stiflingly hot. Already I had noticed how the Connemara people seemed to love a big fire above all things, no matter how warm the weather. The men were sitting with their feet stretched toward the fire as if it were the depths of winter. They had settled their caps on one knee to be ready for departure at a moment's notice, I thought, and still they had a look of repose, as if they intended to stay for a long time. On the floor, just by the front, right-hand leg of each man's chair, a pint glass of black porter was carefully placed. About two inches had been drunk from each glass, but no one seemed in a hurry to get on with his.

I knew at once, of course, that this was the shop. Three great black barrels stood against the far wall. A shelf or two beside them held a little range of groceries—soap, flour, jam, and packets of tea and sugar, as well as a glass jar of sweets. As a shop it was miserable, but if the next one was a couple of miles away, as Mrs. Fahy had said, the women of this place would sometimes be very grateful even for such poor service.

Every head turned to look at me when I appeared in the doorway. Then a small, delicate-looking man who had been sitting on the hob, so close that one would have thought he was being gently roasted, got up and came toward me.

"I'm looking for a place to camp," I said boldly, my blood

still boiling with rage at the treatment I had received from the Scotsman. "There's a fine field over by the big house but a cross-looking fellow with a gun came out and threatened me, and hardly even gave me time to ask."

There was a burst of laughter from the men, which angered me further. I began again, "It's a queer kind of hospitality—"

"Wait, wait!" said the small man. "We were not laughing at you. Indeed, in a certain way you could say we were not laughing at all. It's a queer reception, indeed, and no wonder that you're cross, for that would annoy a saint. Come in and sit down, and you'll see that we'll treat you better in this house, yes, and find you a place to camp as well."

This was all so kindly said that I felt ashamed of my outburst. The little man had a precise way of speaking which somehow went well with him because of his size, though it would have seemed ridiculous with any of his big, hearty visitors. I came slowly into the house and dropped my pack in the corner behind the door. A chair was pulled out for me, and the little man took a mug from the dresser and filled it with milk and placed it solemnly in my hand.

"Drink that up," he said, "and you'll feel calmer. I have a field behind my house, well sheltered enough, and you're welcome to camp in it for as long as you like. My house is not as big as that one you tried to visit, but there's no one will threaten you with a gun. Drink that milk, and then you can be telling us where you come from, and your name and station, as the song says. My name is Carroll—Patsy Carroll they call me, because when I was a small boy there was another Patrick Carroll here, a cousin of my own. He's gone to America long since, but Patsy is still my name."

## ⁊ 5

HERE WAS A FINE PIECE of luck. I could not have hoped for better. It was not hard to guess that Patsy was a bachelor. A thin film of dust floated on top of the milk in my mug, and a layer of dust dimmed the shiny luster jugs on the dresser. Perhaps because he lived alone, Patsy Carroll's shop seemed to be the gathering place for the men of the district. Besides, I knew from Ned Hernon that he was an important man in the plots concerning the deer.

The men were all watching me with interest. There were three of them—as well as Patsy—big, broad, weather-beaten men, dressed in gray tweed trousers and white jackets of the hand-woven tweed called báinín. Under the jackets they wore heavy dark-blue sweaters, and yet the heat of the kitchen seemed not to trouble them at all. Probably the winter's cold that they had to endure gave them a feeling that one could never have too much warmth.

"You're on your holidays," said one of the men. "Fine for you."

"Yes," I said. "I have a little tent and I want to walk through the whole of Connemara at my ease."

"It's beautiful country," said another man. "You won't meet

its like in the world. There's the Grand Canyon and the Rocky Mountains that I saw in the States—those are fine places, but the lakes and the mountains and the sea in Connemara are the best of all."

"Where did you stop last night?" asked the third man. "Maybe you walked out from Galway. It's a long walk but it can be done in a day if you're young and strong."

"I didn't come from Galway." Quickly I had made a decision. "I stayed two nights at the Galway side of Salleen, opposite the house of a man called Ned Hernon, though the land didn't belong to him."

"Ned Hernon? You're the boy that stabbed the shark!"

Patsy Carroll stood up, seized my hand and shook it solemnly. One of the men said, "We heard of you indeed."

"And I heard of you," said I to Patsy, "in Ned Hernon's house last night." He gazed at me directly, with no more expression on his face than a cat. I went on, "They were talking about a man called Michael Joyce, and I'm thinking now that that must be his house over there."

As I said these words, I had an unpleasant sensation of a trap closing in around me. Now I began to wonder if I need have declared myself at all, but immediately my good sense told me that it would have been useless to try to conceal my knowledge. As likely as not, Ned Hernon or one of his sons would visit this house. Once more I resolved to have no more to do with spying as long as I lived. I did not want to retreat now, partly because I was curious to know how it would all end and partly because it seemed to me that only an outsider could succeed in making peace between Michael Joyce and his neighbors. But once that would be achieved, I would be finished with this way of life forever.

"So Ned told you about Michael Joyce," said Patsy gently. "Did he give you any message for me?"

"No," I said, "though I saw him in Salleen as I passed by. He's attending to his sharks today."

The men chuckled, and one said, " 'Tis a great day for Ned, indeed. Two sharks! That's a fine catch. Tell us now, how did you do it?"

"Through knowing no better," I said.

I described my feat, and explained that I had never seen a shark before. All the time while I was talking, I was aware that Patsy Carroll's eyes were on me as if he were trying to see into my brain. They were the round, pale eyes of a cat and they made me horribly uneasy. Though he was following my story, I knew that he was also summing me up and wondering whether Ned Hernon had made a mistake in trusting me. At last it seemed to me that his expression changed, that he had decided in my favor.

When I had finished, the first man who had spoken said, "You'll be taking shark fishing for your trade from this on, I suppose."

"Not if I can find another," I said.

" 'Tis as well," said he. "You couldn't hope for that luck every day."

Then I had to tell my name, and Patsy told me the names of the men that were there. The first one was Martin Folan, the second was Canyon Lee—named Canyon because he was always talking about the Grand Canyon that he saw in America —and the third man was Mike Gavin.

Canyon looked a bit sheepish when his name was explained, but then he said earnestly, "It's a great sight, the Grand Canyon. There isn't its like in the world."

Patsy stood up from the hob and began to build up the fire. When he had surrounded it with tall, black sods of turf, so that it looked like a little volcano, he took a three-legged pot of potatoes, which was ready on the hearth, and hung it from the crane above the fire. Then he said, "Now I'll show you the field for your camp and after that maybe you'll help me to eat those spuds for I have no one else to do it."

His three customers stood up too, each with his pint glass in his hand. With a single movement, they tilted back their heads and poured the porter in a long, uninterrupted stream down their throats. Then they smacked their lips and let out a long "Ah!" one by one, and placed their glasses carefully in a row on top of one of the big barrels. They paced slowly to the door, like a line of ducks, and as each man went out he said, "So long, Patsy. Thanks again."

Patsy chuckled at the expression on my face. "If I didn't give them the hint, they'd be there all night," he said. "Now take your gear and we'll go out."

He led me out by the front door and to a field behind the house. It was a good field to camp in, sloping gently and with a loose stone wall running all around it to give shelter. A five-barred gate led from the laneway into it.

"Sometimes I keep a few bullocks in here," said Patsy, "if the notion takes me, but I haven't had any for a while now. I haven't the health to be minding them, especially in the wintertime."

He watched me detachedly while I erected my tent, but he did not lift a finger to help me. This irritated me. It is quite a feat to get a tent up with no one to hold the poles upright for you. I longed to ask him to do that much at least, but somehow I could not bring myself to say it. The evening sun still glared into the field, since it was no more than seven o'clock, and I sweated under its heat as I hammered the pegs into the hard ground, which had been well trampled by Patsy's bullocks.

When I had quite finished and the tent was standing four-square, he said with approval, "Well done! I couldn't have done better myself." Suddenly he added, "You're not in very good practice. Is this your first time camping out?"

"Yes," I said uneasily. "I'm new to it."

"So I see. Well, practice makes perfect."

He did not ask any more questions. If he had, he would have caught me out at once. I was never much good at spinning a yarn, perhaps because I always imagined that truth and lies were easily visible, like black or white clouds.

When we got back to the kitchen, the potatoes were almost

cooked. With a sharp knife he whacked two chunks off a long piece of bacon and quickly set them to fry on some hot coals on the hearth. Bacon and potatoes seemed to be the diet of Connemara, with cabbage on good days. So far it seemed fine to me, but I wondered how soon I would tire of it if I had it every day of the week.

Patsy took two cracked, chipped plates off the dresser. They had a faded brown pattern of shepherds and sheep on them, which reminded me of the farm in Roscommon where I was supposed to be working. Before leaving home, I had written to my cousin to say I would not be coming after all, so I did not expect any trouble on that score unless my mother took a fancy to visit me there. This thought made me decide to write her a long letter, giving some sort of explanation of my doings and promising to come home rich before long.

"I have paper and envelopes in plenty of my own, though I don't sell them in the shop," said Patsy when I asked him. "They are pretty old now but they're good still. Not many people in the world would be bothered with a letter from me."

He did not say this bitterly but just as a statement of fact.

"Have you no relations at all?" I asked. "Not even in America?"

"Only my namesake, and it would be foolish to write to him for he can hardly read. At least that's how he was when I saw him last, though he may have learned since. He was a bit lazy when he was at home, but maybe when the fright of work was on him he improved. I had two brothers, but they went off to Canada and they forgot about me. I heard they're rich and well, and one of them got to be Lord Mayor or whatever they have out in those wild places. Said I to myself, it would be more fitting for them to come home than for me to go stravaging out there. Them that forget their old home are not worth following."

Now I wondered if he were as detached as he sounded. The thought ran into my mind that this man would be a ruthless enemy. I longed to get him talking about Michael Joyce and the deer, but I was afraid that he would begin to suspect me if I appeared curious. And yet surely it would seem even more strange to avoid the subject altogether.

We worked our way through the potatoes and the bacon, washing them down with dusty milk.

Then Patsy leaned back in his chair and said, "Tonight I'll have to shut the door early and go to bed. It was six o'clock when I got back this morning and it wasn't worth while going to bed then."

I said casually, "It was a long road."

"It was, then, and I'm not used to horses this good while. Horses it had to be for that work. It's a queer thing—when you're riding a horse, you think the horse is doing all the work, but when you get down off him, you feel as if you had walked every inch of the way yourself." He stretched his arms wide. "Stiff and sore in every bone I am."

I helped him to clear off the table and wash our plates in water from the big black kettle. Then he made up the fire with fresh turf, expertly slanting the tops of the sods inward so that the ash would cover the seed of the fire during the night and keep it hot for the next morning. As he was finishing this, I made for the door, not wishing to be given a heavy-handed hint to leave as I had seen him do with his customers.

"A good night's sleep to you," I said.

"And the same to you," said he. "Let you come around in the morning when you wake up and we'll have our tea together. It's not often I have company for breakfast."

He shut the door behind me while I was still on the step. Though I had no wish to stay with him any longer, still I could not help feeling like a cat that has been put out for the night. Behind me, the house had a blank, dead look, perhaps because pots of broad-leaved geraniums grew close against the glass of the windows. But for the firelight, Patsy must have been almost in darkness. The main light in his kitchen had come through the open door, I remembered now.

I moved on out to the road and glanced at the other houses

that were near. On a kitchen chair outside one of them, taking his ease in the last of the sun and puffing his pipe, was Canyon Lee. He looked the very picture of contentment of mind and body, like a man resting after a good day's work, with his eyes closed and his legs crossed. Behind him, a climbing cabbage rose was in bloom against the house wall. A tabby cat lay stretched at full length on the doorstep beside him.

"A grand evening," he said to me when he saw me watching him. "It won't last. We may as well enjoy it while we can."

"Is there bad weather coming?" I asked, thinking of my new tent.

"There's always bad weather coming," said Canyon. "That's the way of the world." He opened his eyes wider to look at the sky. "There's no sign of it yet and it won't come without warning. Are you going for a walk?"

"Yes."

"I'd go with you only I'm tired," he said. "Down to the sea you'll go, I suppose."

"I was thinking of it."

"God speed you," said he. "It's a grand evening for a walk." And he uncrossed his legs and crossed them again with the left one on top this time, to rest it.

I set off along the road, walking on the verge through the thick grass. Beside me, to my right, there was a deep, narrow dyke with a stream bubbling in it. The air was full of lonesome evening sounds—hens clucking, children calling, a doleful cow giving a long, high-pitched bellow, and far off the bark of a dog. As I walked, the sun went down, leaving the sky full of a blue-green light with a reddish glow above the horizon. It would be daylight for a while yet. Not a cloud showed anywhere. The air was still warm and I wondered how long Canyon would sit there to enjoy it.

Feeling casual eyes on me, I made sure to look as if I were merely out to enjoy myself. I ran a few steps now and then, and climbed a stile by the side of the road to see around me, and sometimes I picked up a stone and sent it spinning along in front of me.

In this way I left the village, passed by Michael Joyce's house, and came out on the open road beyond. On my right, the land sloped upward—poor, rocky land with short-bitten grass, crisscrossed with stone walls. On my left, beyond Michael Joyce's smooth, good fields, was the grassy hill I had seen earlier. A brambly laneway ran by the foot of it, leading down toward the sea.

I turned into the laneway. The first part of it was well worn and I soon saw why. In a hundred yards or so I came on a spring well with a paving of stones around it. It was clear and sparkling and its surface twitched and shivered as the water continually rose from its sandy floor. Beyond the well, the brambles grew closer, leaving only a little path in the middle. I followed this, looking for a way onto the hill. I had almost reached the strand before I found it, a place where the brambles thinned and I was able to climb over the wall.

Once I was on the grassy hill, I began to run. The shoulder of the hill came between me and the road so that I knew I could not be seen from the village. Away off above me, almost at the highest point of the hill, there was a scatter of rocks. From there I should be able to see the sea and survey the country all around me.

When I reached the rocks, however, I stopped in surprise. Between two of them there was an opening, like the mouth of a cave, but it did not seem to be a natural one. The rocks had been raised into that position to form door-posts. Their ends were sunk in the earth and heavy stones were placed against them to make sure they stayed upright.

The black doorway did not look inviting. However, since I knew that this must be the old shepherd's hut that Michael Joyce had mentioned, I went cautiously inside.

It was pitch dark at first and I lit a match to see by. This was useless, of course, but I found after a while, when my eyes had adjusted to the dimness, that enough light came from the doorway. The hut was cut deep into the hill, so that several feet of earth formed its roof. This ensured that it was always dry, I suppose, and yet there was an unpleasant smell of damp earth there. It was a single room, more or less circular, where a man might be glad to shelter from a storm or from heavy rain. A few big, flat stones had been placed near the doorway for seats, and on one I found very old and gritty wax drippings from candles.

It was perfectly silent in there and it gave me the creeps. I did not want to wait there for Michael Joyce. I came out and stood in the doorway for a moment, and then I climbed onto the top of the dugout. There below me the sea stretched away for thousands of miles, with nothing between me and America but the three Aran Islands. Very lonesome they looked, three dark-blue curves drawn on the shining sea. The moon was coming up and the sea glittered, but the islands looked black and gloomy. They were too far away for the lights in the houses to show, or perhaps there was a little fog out there which gave them that heavy look.

I knew from the map that there were other islands farther up the coast, but from where I was they were not to be seen. One of them would be Inish Goill, I thought. Perhaps Michael Joyce would know where it was.

There was no wind, but the air had become colder. Overhead the seagulls were squalling. I wondered if they ever slept. From the sea below I heard a horrible moaning, wailing sound, but whether it came from a bird or an animal I could not tell.

The sight of that enormous stretch of water distressed me and I turned my back on it and came down to the dugout again. How long would I wait? It was a lonesome place. I could still hear the doleful moan from the shore. I sat on a stone outside the doorway. Lower down the hill, I saw rabbits come popping out of their burrows and start nibbling the grass, stopping now and then to sit up ridiculously on their hindquarters.

Suddenly, with one movement it seemed, all the rabbits shot into the burrows. I stayed quite still. The moonlight and the last of the daylight together gave everything a grayish look. Then I saw Michael Joyce walking slowly, like a man who has not a care in the world, up the hill toward me.

He saw me when he was a little distance away and began to move faster. I did not go down to meet him, lest someone might happen to be watching or following him. Instead I slipped quickly into the dugout and stood just inside, waiting for him.

When he reached the doorway, the first thing I said to him was, "What is that moaning down on the shore?"

I could hear my voice shake with terror. He laughed softly.

"It's the seals. They gather on the rocks down there on a fine evening and make that sound, like people at a wake, they say."

"I wish I could have seen them. I heard them first when I was up on the hill and the sound seemed to follow me. I was thinking of ghosts—"

"You can't see them from above," he said. "The sea has undercut the cliff and they are in there sitting on the rocks. I'd like to go out in a boat to see them." He paused for a moment and then asked suddenly, "Have you learned anything for me?"

"I've learned why the deer were taken, and who took them, and the name of the place where they are."

"That is a good start." He peered at me in the dimness and I could see a look of respect on his face. "We'll sit down," he went on after a moment. "I wish I could bring you to my own house, but that must wait for another time."

We sat on the cold stones. Then he said, "Why were the deer taken?"

"Because the people think they are useless. There's a land hunger in these parts. The people are angry because you put ornamental animals on land that could have been used for cattle or sheep or horses."

"I wouldn't breed horses in this climate."

"Irish horses are the best in the world," I said hotly. "And not only in green, sheltered places but in Connemara too. The white Arab ponies that were washed ashore off the great Spanish Armada are still bred in Connemara—"

"Easy on, easy on!" he said. "You're right, of course. As I told you in Galway, I didn't want to breed horses. I wanted deer, and not only for an ornament. The meat is a delicacy and the skin is valuable too. It's like keeping cattle."

"The people don't know that."

"Who are these people?"

"Neighbors of yours, and some more distant. I'd like if I didn't have to name them."

"Then how am I to get back my deer?"

"I can name the island where they are."

"Well?"

"Inish Goill, they called it."

But Michael Joyce had never heard of this island. He had good maps, he said, and he had made a study of them to find all the places that his father used to name.

"Especially the islands," he said. "If you live all your life inland, as I did, the sea and the islands are doubly strange and interesting. I'm sure I would remember that name, if I had ever heard it."

"They said it's a long road."

"It could be off the coast of Mayo, farther north."

"No. It's only a night's ride."

"I could call in the Guards."

"You could, indeed, but you told me at the beginning that you don't want to do that. Besides that may be just what the people are waiting for. Then the newspapers will have the story and you'll be called a land-grabber—"

"What is a land-grabber?"

"Your father never told you that?"

"No."

Now I was embarrassed at having to explain this term—it was such an ugly thing. During the Land War in Ireland, when the people refused to pay unjust rents for their land, the bad

landlords evicted the tenants and offered the farms for renting. People were warned not to take those farms, and if anyone did, he became the enemy of the whole neighborhood. His cattle were maimed, his farm boycotted, his life threatened, and he was labelled with the name of "grabber," which came to have an ugly sound. Later, when the Land War was long over and Irish farmers owned their own land at last, the same word cropped up again. This time a grabber meant a different thing: a man who bought a good, big farm which the poor people around had hoped would be divided out among themselves. It was even used if someone bought the land of a foolish farmer who had got into debt and could not pay back to his bank the money he had borrowed. Memories are very long in Ireland. I had often thought it was a silly thing to use the same word that had once been reasonable and true, since now there was no crime in buying a farm wherever one liked, so long as one paid good money for it.

This was Michael Joyce's view, when I had explained. "But I bought the land honestly," he said. "I'm no grabber. I gave a good price for it. It would have been sold to someone else, if not to me."

"Perhaps the people here had hopes that the Land Commission would take it over," I said. "They all knew Colman Donnelly was not working the land, and if you don't use it, after a certain time the Land Commission can force you to sell. Then they divide it out."

"That doesn't make sense to me."

"It makes sense in Ireland," I said, and I added, "I suppose there are a lot of things I wouldn't understand either if I bought a farm in the Argentine."

He gave a short, hard laugh and said, "That's true. Then what should I do?"

"Wait and see if I can discover where Inish Goill is."

"Then we could just go and fetch the deer back. I hope they are not shut in."

"There would be no need. They could be loose on the island, the way they leave cattle or sheep. But there's more to be done than just to fetch them back, if you want to live here in peace."

"Well?" he said impatiently when I hesitated.

"There's that Scotsman you have." I stopped, embarrassed, for it went against my grain to tell of the Scotsman's rudeness.

"Hugh?" said Michael Joyce. "What's wrong with him? He's only here because he knows how to tend the deer."

"It's a pity he's not more civil," I said.

"Is that the way of it? To the best of my knowledge, he had very little to do with the people around here."

"Maybe they don't like that."

"Did they say so?"

"No, but I'm thinking that if he was talking to them the way he did to me, they'll have a few hard things to say about him when he comes up in the conversation. I'd like some time to find out if he has anything to do with the story of your deer."

"What did he say to you? Have you met him already?"

I told him shortly of how Hugh had threatened me with a gun and had called me a name which I had never heard before but which was clearly meant as an insult.

"What is a tripper," I asked, "if it's not a word that should not be explained?"

Michael Joyce gave a little hoot of laughter.

"It's not a very bad word," he said. "In England, and in Scotland too, it seems, when the people come out into the country for a breath of fresh air on a holiday, they're called by that name."

"But he said it as if it were an insult."

"So it is, though it only means someone who takes an outing for the day."

"But are the unfortunate people that live in the towns not to have any fresh air?"

"It's the way of the world, as my father would say," said

Michael Joyce. "People like to keep what they have for themselves."

"Even the fresh air?"

"It's not the air they grudge, it seems, but that the people walk across the land and climb walls—"

"And is that how your Hugh thinks? Let me tell you, Mr. Joyce, even if you never had a herd of deer, there's no place in Ireland where the people would stand for that way of doing things."

"I know he thinks we shouldn't allow anyone to trespass on the land, and he's cross these days on account of the loss of the deer."

I promised to find out what the people thought of the Scotsman, if he had angered them with talk of trespass. I knew they would be furious at the idea that anyone could stop them from walking on the sod of their own country. I had learned so much in the last two days that it seemed certain I would have more news soon.

Michael Joyce asked, "Where have you pitched your tent?"

"Behind Patsy Carroll's shop."

"You don't like this work?" he said after a pause. "Do you want to give it up?"

"No," I said when I had thought it over for a moment. "It's ugly work, but it might turn out well in the long run. There's right on both sides, so far as I can see."

"That's as may be," he said. "I don't see why I should take orders from anyone about what stock I keep on my land. I've never bowed to anyone in my life and I'm not going to start now."

It had got so dark that I could no longer see his face clearly, but I knew by the tone of his voice that he was angry now in a way that he had not been before. We came out of the dugout, and I found it warmer in the night air than it had been underground. The moon lit up the hillside. I saw that the rabbits were out again like little, black, tumbling shadows. In case someone might happen to be watching, I went down the hill alone while he stayed in the darkness of the doorway. When I looked back once, I found that he could not be seen at all.

I crossed the wall and made my way along the lane, with the brambles clawing at me, until I came to the well. There I went faster and I came out onto the road to find Canyon Lee waiting for me.

"I came looking for you," he said, "because you were a long time gone, and when I got this far I heard someone coming up the boreen and I said to myself, that must be the boy that stabbed the shark, for there's no one else would go down there at this hour of the night."

"Why wouldn't they?"

I fell into step beside him, mightly glad that he had no suspicions of me. He answered my question with another. "Did you hear a noise down there?"

"A wailing, moaning, groaning, ologóning—"

"That's it," he said, delighted. "Those were the seals, below on the rocks, and do you know why they were moaning?"

"For the fun of it, I suppose."

"No, faith. It was not. The souls of all the drowned sailors are inside in those seals." He lowered his voice to make it more impressive. "And they do be calling like that at the fall of night, for someone to come down and release them."

"God bless my soul!" said I. "And how can that be done?"

"Easy," said Canyon. "If you go near them, they beckon you with their little front flippers to come closer and closer. They look so quiet and civil, like little elderly gentlemen sitting there, that you go up to them without fear. But if you do, the next thing you know, one of them walks away in the shape of a man, and you're left squatting there on your fishtail, in the shape of a seal, joining in the howling with the rest of them."

"And where does the ghost of the seal go?" I asked, half-believing his story in spite of myself.

"To his heavenly home, where we'll all go some day," said

he casually. We had reached the village now and he said comfortably, "Well, good night to you, and sound sleep. I'll be seeing you tomorrow."

And he pushed open the door of his own house and went inside, leaving me in the darkness.

# ❧ 6

AFTER CANYON'S STORY, I was in no hurry to go into my lonesome tent and lie down for the night. If Patsy's door had been open, I think I would have gone inside and asked him if I might spend the night by the kitchen fire. However, it was shut fast, and as I walked between the houses of the little street, I saw that they were all in darkness.

Now I was thankful for the high, clear moon. I found my way easily into my field and quickly lit a candle which I placed on top of the cooking-stove. Its yellow flame was a comfort and I kept it alight until I began to feel a drowsy warmth in my sleeping bag. Then I blew it out and was soon asleep.

In the morning I wondered at my uneasiness of the night before. It was the hens that woke me, boasting about their new-laid eggs. There must have been a dozen of them behind every house, and the air was full of their sharp, clear voices. Sometimes two or three of them were at it together and their top notes, each on a different pitch, made a deafening chorus. By comparison the cocks' crowing sounded restrained and orderly. Between them all, there was no fear that anyone would sleep late in that village.

Patsy's kettle was almost boiling when I reached his kitchen.

There were two big flowery mugs ready on the table and a fine, gold-crusted loaf of soda-bread.

"Sarah John brings me a loaf every morning in time for my breakfast," said Patsy, "and I suppose that's why I don't die of starvation, for I'd never go to the bother of making it myself. Sarah John is Canyon's wife—you remember Canyon that you met here last night."

"Yes, I remember him."

"Well, Sarah is a fine woman, the kind you could have a bit of trust in. There aren't many of them in the world."

He said this rather sourly, so that I wondered what the women of the world had done to him. I said, "I met Canyon again last night when I was coming back from the sea. He told me I was lucky not to be turned into a seal."

Patsy laughed. "Canyon is full of the old stories," he said. "He has nothing else to think of, I suppose. He was on a whaling ship in Canada for a while and he told us he saw seals as big as cows with long white fur that you could dress a king in. He's a terrible man for the stories. He made a fortune out in those places, though, so that he doesn't have to work no more, as the song says."

Feeling that I ought to defend Canyon, I said, "I didn't believe what he said about the seals hereabouts, but I know there are white seals with long fur in the far north. I've read about them."

"As big as a cow?" Patsy asked.

"Almost as big as a small cow."

Patsy considered this. Then he said, as he put the teapot on the table, "I'm not an ignorant man. I never traveled much, because of my health, but I always liked to meet the people that did, and to hear stories from them about what they saw. But they should be true stories. There are enough wonders in the world without making them up. And when a man starts off to tell you about something he saw with his own eyes, he has no right to put in things that a three-year-old child wouldn't believe."

Patsy looked so angry that I guessed Canyon had been in the habit of pulling his leg, perhaps embroidering true accounts of things he had seen to make a good story. I could imagine that it would be a temptation to imitate Ulysses with tales of dragons and one-eyed giants and islands where no one ever grows old.

"Did you see e'er a sign of that bad-tempered Scotsman last night?" Patsy asked while we were eating. " 'Tis a wonder you were let go near the sea at all, between himself and his gun! I said to him, ''tis a dangerous thing to show a gun in these parts, for you might get worse than you'd offer.' Oh, it's no harm to talk straight to the like of him."

"That sort of talk didn't improve his temper, I'm sure," I said casually, glad that I had not had to bring up the subject myself.

"It did not, then," said Patsy. " 'Are you threatening me?' said he. 'What else am I doing?' said I. 'I'm walking this land all my life and I'm not going to stop for any Sassenach.' That made him mad altogether. 'I'm no Sassenach,' said he. 'I'm a Scot.' 'Then you ought to know better,' said I to him, and I went on with my walk. Out on the hill I was, where I often used to go for a blow of air. But a funny thing, though I defied him and said I'd please myself, I never went out that way since."

"Does he ever come in for a pint of porter?"

"Never. I don't know what he does when he has a thirst on him. He's an unnatural creature, whatever way you look at him."

"Maybe he drinks milk," I suggested solemnly.

" 'Tis like what he'd do," said Patsy.

When we had finished breakfast, I offered to fetch a can of water for him as I saw he had used the last of it to refill the kettle.

"Do that," he said, "and I'll be milking the cow in the meantime."

I took the can and went outside. As I passed Canyon's door,

a woman called out to me from inside, "Hold on there!" Wait a second and I'll be with you!"

I waited, and in a moment out came a wide-skirted, humorous-looking woman carrying a can in her hand.

"You're the boy that stabbed the shark," she said. "Oh, that was a great gaisge! You'll be the talk of west Connacht for a year and a day."

I could see that that was going to be my name from now on.

She said, "They call me Sarah John. John was my father— not John Tadhg but John Peter. Canyon is my husband—that rascal you met last night. He told me that you have a little bothán of a tent in Patsy Carroll's field where he used to keep the bulls. Tell me, now, aren't you afraid to be out there on your lone in the dead of night?"

"No."

"Ah, you're a hardy boy and no doubt about it. I'd be afraid of my mortal life. Wait there now for a second," she said suddenly as we reached the last house in the village which stood a little back from the road at the end of a short boreen. "I must call Maggie Tom."

And she let out a bellow that nearly lifted me off the ground with fright: "Maggie Tom! Maggie Tom!"

A woman appeared in the doorway and shouted back, "Ara, what's on you?"

"Going to the well I am," Sarah yelled. "Let you come along with us!"

"All right so," Maggie called, and her voice was pitched like a seagull's, as if Sarah were at least a mile away. "Wait now till I put the sow and the bonavs back in the field."

We waited, and heard her voice saying, "Hurrish, hurrish, hurrish! Get in there, ye devils! Hurrish, let ye. Hurrish!"

The gate of the field clanked and she went into the house for her water can. Then she came flying down the boreen toward us—a tall, thin woman with dark hair piled on top of her head and held there with a comb which had glittering diamondlike stones in it.

"The pigs are never satisfied," she said. "If himself puts them in one field, they want to be in another. If he moves them to the other field, they put their eye on a new place. They have me vexed, so they have. They have my heart broken. Bad manners to them!"

"Don't say that about the blessed animals," said Sarah hurriedly. "With God's help you'll be rich at Christmas from them."

" 'Tis true for you."

Now we had to go faster, because Maggie Tom had long legs and she strode like a man. Very soon we came up with a woman who was walking by herself. She was not wearing the long red flannel skirt and checked apron that my two companions wore. It was beginning to be a warm day and I wondered how they were able to endure those clothes. The other woman had a flowered cotton dress and she looked fine and cool. She had a water can in her hand and was obviously on the same business as ourselves. As we passed her by, Sarah said shortly, "Good day to you, ma'am."

The woman turned a thin, frightened face to us and said very quietly, "Good day."

We passed on silently, leaving her to walk by herself. When we were a hundred yards or more ahead of her, Maggie said, "As grand as she is with her water taps and her bath, she has to go to the well for a drop to drink like the rest of us. I wish I could like her. But there's nothing hearty about her. Maybe 'tisn't her fault. Maybe I wouldn't be too hearty myself if I was looking at Colman Donnelly's cold-water face every day of my life."

"She's every bit as bad as him," said Sarah. " 'Twould be a pity to spoil two houses with them. If she would leave the door open, same. How can you walk up to a house that has the door always shut? 'Tisn't Christian. Colman's father, God rest him,

never had the door shut, though he was an old rasper in other ways."

"Leave them to God," said Maggie tolerantly, "and He'll play the devil with them."

Then I had to tell them how I had stabbed the shark—every move of it. It was the second time I had told it in twenty-four hours and I found I was getting good at it. I began to put in little details that I had left out before, and I had to restrain myself from inventing a few things that had never happened at all. It would have sounded good to say that the shark had snapped a piece out of the sleeve of my sweater as I struck at him, or that he had rolled his eyes wickedly and showed his teeth like a dog the moment before, or that he had lashed the currach perilously with his tail. However, even the stark truth brought out so many exclamations of astonishment that I was satisfied.

Maggie Tom said over and over, "Oh, isn't it the sport! Oh, isn't it the devil himself!"

Sarah was probably accustomed to hearing about marvels, from Canyon. She was a bit quieter in her admiration, but both agreed that I was a great hero.

We came to the well, filled our cans, and started back along the lane a little more slowly now. At the mouth of it we met Mrs. Donnelly again and she looked as if she had been waiting for us to leave the well before she would go down herself. Again Sarah and Maggie greeted her shortly and they did not mention her in their talk on the road home.

Maggie left us at her own house, and Sarah and I walked together the rest of the way. Before she left me, she made me promise that I would visit her in the evening when she would have all her work done.

"Pigs and calves and chickens and cows are a lot worse than children to look after," she said. "All day long I'm drawing feed to them, but sure, they're worth it in the end, I suppose, and what else would I be doing with my time? Long ago I used

99 🖎

to think I'd have a grand easy life when the children would be grown up and gone away from me."

I thought of Canyon, sitting all afternoon in Patsy Carroll's and all evening outside his own door, but I did not like to suggest that she might spend at least some of her time as he did.

As I reached Patsy's door, I heard voices inside, and sure enough there was Canyon already with his legs stretched out to the fire. Patsy was sitting on the hob, with his feet drawn in from the heat. There was no glass at Canyon's feet this time, as I suppose it was too early in the day. I crossed the kitchen and put the can of water on the bench beside its dipper.

Canyon said heartily, "And how is the brave hero this morning?"

I said that I was well, and had slept well and long.

"We all slept long," said Canyon. "There were doings this morning while we were all in bed, as I was just telling Patsy."

Now I saw that he was in a state of great excitement, in spite of his sitting so quietly. While he talked, he kept giving little hoots of laughter, and his voice was louder than was needed even in a big kitchen. Now and then Patsy would say, "Easy, there, Canyon! We're right here beside you."

And Canyon would try for a while to keep his voice down but he could never do it for long.

It was a strange story. Canyon had heard it from Mary Paddy, who worked in Michael Joyce's house. She was a quiet woman from Rosmuc, who was very friendly with everyone in the village. She had come over to Canyon's house while we were at the well, to tell him what had happened.

She had a room over the kitchen in the big house. Hugh, the Scotsman, had a fine loft all fixed up as a bedroom, over where the carriages were kept in the old times, though, as Canyon said, there was never a road fit for a carriage in that part of Connemara. Hugh had a key to the back door of the house, and at the dawn of the morning, while she was still in bed, he had come up the kitchen stairs and tapped at Mary's door. His face was white and his eyes were staring with the fright that was on him, she said. He told her that he was leaving immediately, that he wanted to see no one, that he would not awaken Michael Joyce and tell him what had happened lest he might be persuaded to stay as much as an hour longer, that he was getting out of Connemara as fast as he could, and that he hoped never to lay eyes on it nor on its godless people again as long as he lived.

"What happened?" I asked as Canyon paused for breath. "Only yesterday he looked ready to fight the world."

"Mary couldn't get much sense out of him about that," said Canyon. "Someone came in the night and threatened him— she thought it was a few of us here but I told her we hadn't done any such thing. He spoke of guns, and something about the old times, and how his kind was treated then, and a whole lot of nonsense she couldn't follow. And then he said he was taking the roan horse and he'd leave him in the Royal Hotel's yard in Galway, and he was going to get the train and the boat to Scotland and never set foot in Ireland again. He's no loss, that's certain, and we should be thankful to whoever put the run on him."

"I'm not sure it will do any good," said Patsy.

"Of course it will, man," said Canyon positively. "Now is the time to start writing the letters."

"What letters?" I asked, though if I had waited a moment, I should have guessed the answer.

"Letters to Michael Joyce," said Patsy, "to tell him to take his deer off the land and either put it to some Christian use or give it up to them that will."

I could say nothing to this, of course. If I had said that deer are useful animals like cattle and that their hides and meat could be sold in the same way, I would have been suspected at least of lack of sympathy.

Patsy was looking very worried. "I don't like this," he said. "Threats with guns are not needed. That was decided. We all agreed. I'd like to know who those men were, that took the law into their own hands."

I thought this a strange thing to say, considering what he and his friends had been doing. It had occurred to me that I knew who had frightened the Scotsman away. While they discussed the whole question and guessed at the various possibilities, I was remembering Ned Hernon's father, how angry he had been at the weakness of the plot against Michael Joyce. He had suggested slaughtering the deer and he had also said that in the old times they would not have stopped there. It seemed very likely that some of the old warriors had taken a hand in the matter without consulting anyone.

The discussion might have gone on all day if another man had not come in. His arrival stopped the other two as if they had suddenly been struck dumb. He was a man I had never seen before, of middle height, with one shoulder higher than the other, giving him a mean, sidling look. He was pale-faced, and looked as if he were not very healthy. I could see at once that he was not accustomed to spending his time at outdoor work as his neighbors did. His hands especially betrayed him. They were soft and white and smooth.

Sure enough, after a moment, Patsy said, "Well, Colman, it's you that's in it. A fine day we have."

"It is, it is, indeed," said Colman. "A good day for the woodcock."

"It could be, for them that have the time to go after them," said Canyon casually, as if he were a very busy man himself.

Colman Donnelly looked from one of us to the other uneasily and then asked, "What news have you?"

"The Scotsman is gone," said Patsy shortly.

Colman gave a high, nervous giggle—an unexpected sound which made me look at him with a new curiosity. Until now I had not thought very much about his part, in the whole business. The land had been his, and he had sold it to Michael Joyce. He had been blamed, Mrs. Fahy said, for not making a success of the fine shop and farm that his father had left him, but I had imagined that he was treated with friendly contempt by his neighbors. They must have trusted him, I thought, or

they would not have hidden the deer on his land. Now it occurred to me that it was a strange thing to keep the deer so near home.

Colman was saying, "May all the bad luck of the year go with him. Why did he go?"

"Someone threatened his life."

"Who?"

"I'd like to know that," said Patsy. "Did you happen to see anyone on the road late last night?"

"Only Canyon, here, and the boy."

This was a nasty little shock. I had not seen a soul as we walked back to the village last night. Colman seemed quite friendly to me, however, as he could not have been if he had seen my meeting with Michael Joyce. Last night the moon had been so bright that the strong shadows could have concealed a regiment.

"We were thinking it would be no one from here," said Patsy. "Everyone agreed that there were to be no threats, at least not of that sort."

"Then maybe it was the Salleen men," Colman said.

"They wouldn't be likely to do it either," Canyon said, "but now that it's done, I'm thinking it was a good night's work."

"So long as the deer are safe," said Colman.

"They're safe enough where they are," Patsy said impatiently. "There's no one will touch the deer. They'll never think of looking for them where they are now."

"True for you, I suppose," said Colman doubtfully. "It's well we shifted them from my place, at least."

Patsy looked at him directly and said, "Yes."

I sensed some undercurrent in this conversation but I could not make out what it was—contempt for Colman, perhaps, or even distrust of him. I thought this was not quite fair. Colman spoke softly and apologetically but he seemed to be just as clever as either of the other two. The speed with which he had suggested that the Salleen men had been responsible for frightening away the Scotsman convinced me of this.

Canyon was saying, "Now that the Scotsman is gone, it will be easier to take away a few more of the deer if we want to. That fellow was like a hen minding chickens. I'm telling you, we should be thankful and very thankful to whoever did last night's work."

"Maybe so," said Patsy reluctantly. "I'd better go down and see Ned Hernon and talk it over with him. Ned has good ideas."

"I'll go with you to shorten the road, if you like," said Colman.

"There's no need, thanks all the same," said Patsy. "Myself and the horse will be company for each other."

Colman gave his strange giggle again but he looked rather angry, as if he had wanted very much to be in the conference with Ned. I thought Patsy had been rather too short with him, and not very civil in suggesting that a horse would be as good company.

Canyon said, "You'll be wanting the gray pony so?"

"Yes," Patsy said, "if he's not working."

"Sure how can he work when I'm not working?" said Canyon. "Though I'm thinking he has more of a mind for it than I have myself." He stood up lazily and slowly, as if he had done a hard morning's work already, and rambled to the door.

When he had gone outside, Colman said, "Canyon always takes his time. He never has anything on his mind. He'll bury us all, he's so easy-going. It's a great way to be."

He sounded genuinely envious and indeed he himself seemed a very uneasy person. Patsy made no reply, and after a moment Colman stood up and said, "Well, I'll be going. I'll see you later when you have a bit of news."

"Good day to you, then," said Patsy calmly.

I dared not ask Patsy why he had treated Colman in this way. For all I knew, I was going to get the same myself any moment. However, Patsy looked quite friendly as he said, "I'll be gone till the evening, I'm sure. Anyone that has a thirst on him can wait for me or else take a two-mile walk over to

Drake's place. I'm thinking the most of them will wait. Are you any good to milk a cow?"

I said that I was; that I did it every day at home.

"Then you can milk mine in the evening if I'm not back by six o'clock. And don't let the fire out. That fire hasn't gone out in a hundred years. You'll find spuds in the bag there by the back door and you can boil them for your dinner, and there's a piece of bacon from yesterday. And lock the door any time you're out of the house. It's not my neighbors I'm thinking of, but the tinkers come around sometimes, and if they do, they'll have high jinks with the barrels of porter."

"Do they come this way often?" I asked, thinking of the Burkes.

"Not too often," he said. "There's hardly anyone here that needs to buy a horse or a donkey. If he can't breed his own, there's always a neighbor with one to spare. And our pots are mostly made of iron so there isn't much to bring the tinkers here."

I promised to keep a sharp eye out for them in any case, and to milk the cow if necessary. While he was telling me where to find her, and describing her so that I would be sure to milk the right cow, we heard the pony's hoofs on the gravel outside the door. Patsy went out at once and climbed awkwardly into the saddle. It was a gray Connemara pony, long-legged and slim, with a wild, intelligent eye. It danced a little on the gravel, obviously looking forward to the exercise.

Canyon kept his hold on the bridle while he said, "Keep him to the road and he'll jog along easily. If you put him on the edge, he'll go into a canter the minute he feels the grass under him and he won't stop till he gets to Salleen."

"That's all right. We understand each other," said Patsy.

Canyon let the reins go, and the pony instantly shook his head until the bridle rattled, and then he took off down the road at a fast trot.

"Patsy is too light," Canyon said, looking after them. "What that pony needs is a good twelve-stone weight on his back.

That would make a quiet boy of him. Well, I'd best get something done around the place."

He moved slowly off in the direction of his own house, as reluctant for work as the horse had been eager.

I knew exactly how I wanted to spend the rest of the day. Those deer of Michael Joyce's were the reason why I was here. I had heard about them over and over for a week. I knew what trouble they had caused, how the law of the land had been broken because of them, and a man's life threatened, and now more plots were being worked out concerning them. And in all my life I had never laid eyes on a deer. There seemed to be something almost disgraceful in this, since they were the subject of so much talk—almost as if I had never seen a donkey or a cow.

I was determined that before the day was out, I would find Michael Joyce's herd of deer and have a good look at them. I knew nothing about where they were, except that it was not near the sea.

Quickly I locked the door of Patsy Carroll's shop and put the key in my pocket. Trying to look idle, I walked westward along the village street. No one had time to bother with me. The morning's work was underway and the women were all busy. Up from the road, on the side away from the sea, I saw a little school which I had not noticed before. Its door stood open now and a faint humming noise came from inside, probably from the smallest people learning arithmetic tables. It reminded me horribly of all the things I wanted to learn, that could not be learned in a school like this.

A little beyond Michael Joyce's house, a narrow side road led off to the right among the fields. I could see for a long distance how it wound between low stone walls, mounting all the time. I turned into it and found it had signs of being used regularly by donkey and horse carts. Here and there as I walked along, at places where the road had been specially widened, I came upon great ricks of good black turf, with the aroma of a hundred winter fires in it. Then there were no more stone walls, but bogland stretching away on my left as far as I could see, and on my right a huge expanse of rough grassy land, scattered with rocks and fenced in with strong wire netting.

The fencing was so unusual in this part of the world that I paused to look at what it enclosed. Probably in Connemara it would pass for reasonably good land. Brambles grew here and there around the rocks, and hazel and furze in patches.

Then I saw the deer. They were in a loose herd, browsing at a clump of hazel bushes, moving gently along as they nibbled. They were quite a long way off, perhaps four hundred yards, so that I could not see them properly. Their beautiful pale color and their branching antlers were so wonderful to me that I could not take my eyes off them. I longed to get closer, but there was no hope of climbing that fence. In any case I guessed that they would not wait for me. Even now, a few of them had lifted their heads nervously and were gazing in my direction. I stood perfectly still, trying by sheer force of will to make my eyes see better than they were able to do. I was so concentrated on this impossible task that I paid no heed to the sound of light footsteps approaching, until I heard Colman Donnelly's voice beside me say softly, "Strange-looking beasts, aren't they?"

"They're beautiful," I said. "I wish I could see them nearer."

"They're too shy," Colman said. "You have to know their ways."

"How were they ever able to catch the ones that were taken away?"

I had almost called them the ones that were stolen.

"Canyon did it," Colman said. "He learned something about them in Canada, if it's true for himself. Canyon would chance anything. If you ask him will he be able to do it, he always says the same thing, that he learned how when he was in Canada."

Again Colman had surprised me with his way of thinking. His soft voice and slightly shifty look made it easy to see him as

something of a simpleton, and I wondered if his neighbors had been deceived by this. I said, "Did Canyon go with the deer to Inish Goill too?"

Colman gave a queer, soft little laugh. After a pause, he said, "No. Only Patsy Carroll and Morgan Curran went. Morgan came up from Salleen to do the job. They took them to my place first, for a few days. They were very secret about it. No one was allowed to come up this road at all that evening, even before it was dark, nor to see them on their way. Up there over the mountain they went. It's a rough road but good enough for horses."

He pointed to where the road continued over the hill, evidently dropped into a valley, and then climbed again to where I could see it straggling up the side of the mountain beyond.

# ≥ 7

AT LAST I KNEW IN WHICH direction the deer had gone. Still I
was puzzled by one thing. I asked, "Where is this island, Inish
Goill? How could they have gone there over the mountain?
Surely that road leads away from the sea?"

"Of course it does. The nearest sea in that direction must be
Sligo Bay, if you don't count Killary Harbor. Inish Goill is on
Lough Corrib."

I had never thought of this, though of course I had always
known about the wonderful lake that stretched north of Galway for thirty miles. I knew it was dotted with islands, but it
had not occurred to me that the people at the seacoast would
know them well enough to make use of them when necessary.
It was no wonder that Michael Joyce had not recognized the
name.

"So that's why they said it was a long road," I said.

"It is a long road," said Colman, "and they had to go at
night so as not to be seen. Anyone that met them would think
he was seeing ghosts."

"They must have tied the deer on a long leading rope."

"Yes, that would be the only way."

I tried to imagine the scene, but it was impossible to think of
those wild creatures being led like horses in a string. Yet Mi-

chael Joyce had said that the Scotsman had had names for them all, and that they were quite tame with him.

"They're easy animals," Colman said casually, as if he had heard what I was thinking. "I went up to see them when they were on my land and I was thinking I'd like to keep a few myself. They look after themselves. You don't have to do a single thing for them."

"I thought you had sold all your land," I said, glad of the chance of finding out about this.

"I kept some in another place a few miles from here, and some down by my new house," said Colman. And then he added with sudden bitterness, "A couple of wild fields! This was all mine." He waved his arm wide. "Every bit you can see from here, every blade of grass was all mine and should be yet."

"But you sold it," I said mildly.

"Rights go deeper than buying and selling," he said, still in that venomous tone. "This land was my father's, and his father had it before him." He stopped suddenly as if he realized that he was not talking good sense. In a quieter tone he said, "Come down from here. It doesn't do me good to look at it."

I could understand that this would be true. As we walked down the hill together, I could not bear to look at him, lest I might see the face that would match the way he had spoken.

After a few minutes he said, "You have nothing to do for the day, since Patsy is gone. Come into my house and my wife will make tea for us."

It would have been impossible to refuse. I did not want to spend another minute in his company if I could help it, and yet I knew that I must not miss this chance of getting some more insight into the whole business. I was not quite sure what I distrusted about Colman Donnelly. There was something in his very nearness to me that made my flesh creep, though he had been very civil to me.

His house was well outside the village, on the road to the west. A short laneway led up to it, and now I saw that it was almost at the end of this laneway that we had overtaken Colman's wife that same morning.

At the top of the lane we came to a neatly kept, low, slated house. Though its door was shut, as Sarah and Maggie had complained, to me it did not look as forbidding as it did to them. Perhaps this was because we had many such houses in my part of the country, with brightly polished brass knockers and net curtains on the windows. The shut door, the net curtains through which you could see without being seen, seemed monstrous to the people of Connemara—almost as if you did not trust your neighbors.

During the next half-hour, however, I went through such fidgets that I stopped making excuses for the Donnellys. We had tea in a stiff little parlor that had china ornaments and brass vases and animals in every inconvenient place, so that I was afraid to let out my breath for fear of knocking them over. I could not imagine Sarah John in this parlor at all. Perhaps she would be brought to the kitchen if she were to come for a visit. But I could not imagine "the thin one" having a fine comfortable kitchen that you would be glad to stretch your legs in either. She seemed to be thin both in mind and body, I thought, and I was mighty glad when I was able at last to get up and say I would be going. She looked disappointed.

"You'll come again," she said eagerly. "You'll be around here for a few days at least."

She was lonely, I could see, and I felt mean that I did not pity her. As I walked down the lane to the road, I could feel my mouth tighten sourly as I imitated in my mind her close way of talking: "Is that so?" "Indeed yes!" "It could be." And in spite of their friendliness, I was already planning a dozen excuses for never crossing their threshold again.

Back at Patsy's house, I made up the fire and put on a few potatoes to boil, thinking as I did so that except for sleeping outside I was suffering very few of the inconveniences of my present way of life. So far, I had done very little outdoor cooking, which pleased me very well. I found the bacon in the musty press by the back door, and when my potatoes were boiled, I made a fine meal at the kitchen table. When I had cleared it away, there was nothing to do but sit down and wait for Patsy.

The afternoon seemed very long. Some of Patsy's usual customers dropped in when they saw the door standing open. Mike Gavin, whom I had met the evening before, said with a longing look at the barrels, "Sure, Patsy won't mind if we milk a pint for ourselves while he's away."

"He said no one was to touch the barrels," I said, "and that he'd be back in the evening, and that I was to say that if anyone had a thirst on him he could walk two miles to Drake's place."

"I can nearly hear him saying that," said Mike sourly.

I thought he was going to ask me to draw him a pint all the same, or that he would do it himself. I would not have been able to stop him. However, he sat in front of the fire looking resigned, and kept me company for an hour without ever mentioning the porter again. Two or three others came in then and he undertook to explain that they must live with their thirst until Patsy came back.

After a while I was sorry that I had decided to spend the whole afternoon indoors, tending the fire and listening to the slow chat of Patsy's neighbors, but I had neither the skill nor the courage to show them the door as he would have done. I did not learn very much, because though they spoke of the deer from time to time, it was always indirectly, almost as if they did not really believe in their existence. I could see that they thought them outlandish animals, not to be taken too seriously by strong, hearty men like themselves who were used to dealing with wild and unmanageable cattle and horses.

The kitchen was full of pipe smoke by six o'clock. The door stood open and the sun poured in on the dusty floor. As there was no sign of Patsy, I said I would go out and find his cow and milk her.

Martin Folan said, "I'll come with you. She's a crotchety cow, like Patsy himself."

There was a great laugh at this, but for all that, I could see that they were somewhat in awe of Patsy. I judged that they intended to wait for him—to be there when he came back from Salleen with his news. Several more men had come in, so that there was not room for them all to sit down. The benches along the walls and the two hobs were all occupied, as well as the few chairs.

I was glad to get out into the fresh air of the yard. Martin led me to the field where the cow was. She was a little black Kerry cow, very lively. I would have liked to milk her myself, but Martin said, "Give me that can!"

I handed it over, and in a second he was down on one knee with his head against the cow's flank, sending the milk singing into the can. The cow switched her tail and chewed the cud, and showed no sign of the bad character that Martin had given her.

As we got back to the house with the full can, Canyon arrived. Martin put the can on top of one of the barrels as there was no place for it on the floor where it would be safe from a chance kick.

Canyon said, "Patsy is coming over the road now, and there's someone with him."

Instantly everyone stood up and went outside to peer along the road toward Galway. Canyon winked at me, picked up the biggest and best chair in the room, placed it with its back to the wall beside the fire, facing the door, and arranged himself comfortably in it. A minute later, the sound of hoofs could be heard approaching. There was a murmur of voices as Patsy and his companion dismounted. I stood in the recess of the back door, in the hope that I would thus remain unnoticed to hear what would be said. Then Patsy came into the kitchen, closely followed by John Hernon.

Patsy looked very tired. All the same, he could not sit down until he had drawn a pint of porter for every man there. Several of the men offered to help, but he did not accept. He was very polite, but I could see that he had trained his customers perfectly and would not give way no matter what the conditions. At last he took a very small glass for himself and went to sit on the hob which had been left free for him.

John Hernon came over and stood silently beside me, nudging me with his elbow in the ribs by way of a greeting. It seemed that our place was in the corner out of the way, while our elders were talking. John was a complete contrast to Patsy. The long ride from Salleen seemed to have given him energy. His eyes were bright and he walked in a lively way, almost as if he were dancing. He looked at me with a delighted grin, as if we were in some marvelous scheme together. Without knowing why, I felt a strange sense of excitement in my fingers and toes, making them tingle.

"What wisdom did you learn from the men of Salleen?" Canyon asked when Patsy had taken a small sip of his porter.

"Wisdom they haven't," Patsy said, "so they can't teach it. It was them that frightened off the Scotsman."

"The devils!"

"They're great men in Salleen!"

"They're not afraid of God nor man!"

These remarks, in tones of admiration, were not made very loud, so as not to disagree too much with Patsy's view. He heard them, of course.

"They have courage, to be sure, but not too much sense," he said in his light, judicial voice. "Maybe when we're their age, we won't have a lot of sense either."

"Their age?"

"What age? Aren't we all the one age?"

"It was the old fellows that did it," said Patsy. "The grandfathers that still have their old guns in the rafters, waiting for the day when they'll be useful again. They came up by night on horseback with their rifles across the saddles—"

"How many of them?" Canyon asked.

"Three."

"You made it sound like an army."

"It was enough. They woke up the poor Scotsman and frightened the living wits out of him with stories about what they did to the Black and Tans. They told him he was for the road in the dawn of the morning. They had a wonderful time. They're all in bed today with hot water bottles and glasses of punch, and their womenfolk giving out to them about their foolishness. But they look very pleased with themselves. I was around to visit them all."

"Who are they? Who are the heroes?"

"Jock Feeney, Roddy Faherty, and Ned Hernon's father, old Tadhg."

"They rode here from Salleen and home again in the dead of night?"

All the men were chuckling with appreciation of the old fellows' exploit. Not a single one spared a thought for the poor Scotsman's terror. I tried to imagine how it would feel to be awakened in the middle of the night, in a foreign country, by three aged desperadoes with guns, and ordered to leave at the crack of dawn. But remembering how the Scotsman had threatened me, I found I had not much pity for him either.

"We spent the day talking," Patsy said, "and we were thinking that Michael Joyce may get a bit cross when he finds his herdsman is gone, especially when he hears why. And we were thinking he may send in to Galway for the Guards; if those fellows come, they'll want to know the whereabouts of every man in this parish. So the best place for every man is on his own hob. At the same time, someone must go to Inish Goill and see how the deer are faring. If anything happens to those deer, we'll be in the wrong in a way that we don't want to be. We agreed they were to be kept safe."

He paused expectantly. Various voices said, "Yes. That's right." "They're his property." "They must be kept safe."

"So Ned Hernon thought of a plan," said Patsy. "His son John, that I brought with me, and Peter Regan, that stabbed the shark, can go off together. No one will take a tack of notice of two boys. They won't be missed from here because this is not their place of residence. And they have as much sense between them as any one man of ourselves."

This seemed a doubtful sort of compliment. John Hernon nudged me and whispered, "We'll be off tonight. We'll bring the little tent. I'm dying to sleep in that little tent!"

I was delighted at the thought of this expedition, you may be sure. I could have told the company that Michael Joyce was not likely to send for the Guards, but of course there could be no question of saying this. How should I know Michael Joyce's mind? And in any case, I would not have said a word that would have reduced the need for my setting off with John for Inish Goill.

Now all the men turned around to look at us, where we still stood in the angle of the doorway. They seemed to me to be assessing us too closely, and I hoped that they would not see my shrinking fear that I would be found out as a spy in their midst. All the eyes were friendly, however. With one accord they lifted their glasses solemnly and drank to us. Then they turned back to Patsy.

"How is the pony?" Canyon asked. "Did he rest himself while you were in Salleen?"

"Ned turned him into the field. We took the saddle off him, and the bridle, and Ned lent me a headstall so that I could catch him again. Oh, he had a fine rest."

"Then he'll be ready for a night's work," said Canyon. He chuckled. "Work he wanted, and now he's getting it."

"And Ned's horse is in fine fettle too," Patsy said. "He'll be well able for the journey."

I began to wonder what length this journey was going to be. All night to get there and back, Patsy had said. So long as I had John Hernon with me, I did not care. But we were not to come back at once, since we were to bring the tent. I might have asked a lot of questions if I had been as much at ease as I looked. Instead I kept very quiet, waiting for instructions from John or from Patsy.

A few minutes later, Canyon stood up and said, "Well, we'd best be off. The boys will be wanting to eat before they start. We'll say good luck to the two of ye and may ye meet no one worse than yourselves on the road."

One by one the men finished their drinks and went out. Then Canyon put his head in through the door again to say, "I'll take the horses over to my place and give them a drink. And listen to me, young lads! Don't forget to let them drink every few miles. My fellow likes plenty of water. It's well he never heard of porter."

We heard the horses' hoofs crush the soft sand as he led them away. Patsy took a parcel out of his pocket.

"Rashers I bought in Salleen," he said. "I'll be cooking them while you get the tent rolled up."

We darted outside, glad of a breath of air after being cooped up with the pipe smoke which had all seemed to roll over toward our refuge by the back door.

"As long as I live, I'll never smoke a pipe," I said. "They'd poison the whole parish, so they would."

John was over the wall into my field in a flash and walking admiringly around and around my tent. Together we dismantled it and rolled it up tightly. The space where it had been looked very small and desolate.

"We'll hang these bundles from the saddles," John said. "There was talk of Morgan Curran coming first, but I said it would be better to leave it to us. Patsy Carroll gave it all out there as if it was his own idea, but it was I that thought of you and myself going together."

"Did anyone say we should bring more of the deer with us?" I asked.

"It was thought of, but they said they won't do it yet. I'd like that fine, to be trotting them over the mountain."

"In the dark?"

"That would make it all the more fun."

I agreed, for the sake of my reputation as a tough, courageous man.

Patsy had a panful of rashers and eggs ready when we got back to the kitchen. We had Sarah John's bread with them, and this reminded me that I had promised to visit her in the evening.

"She won't expect you," Patsy said when I told him. "The whole parish will know you're on other business tonight."

We washed our meal down with foul-tasting strong tea and some of the new milk, straight from the can.

Patsy said, "You'd best take the rest of the bread with you. That's hungry country, up by the lake. When the daylight comes, ye can go onto the island and count the deer, and make sure they are in their health. After that ye can come home."

Patsy gave John two blankets to sleep in, and we made a tight roll of these and of my sleeping bag. When Canyon led the horses to the door again, we attached these bundles firmly to the saddles so that they lay in front of us. In this way we could be sure of holding them steady and not frightening the horses. Canyon was very particular about this, but he said, "That pony has carried some mighty queer things in his day."

When we were ready to go, they still made us wait until the sun had gone down before we were allowed to set out on our journey. We would have the moon later on, they said, so we would not want for light. It seemed an age until we climbed into the saddles at last. By that time, most of the company had come back to see us off. As we trotted along the road to the west, I looked back and saw them all crowding into Patsy Carroll's house.

"They'll be there half the night," John said when I told him. "It's well we won't be in with them, swallowing their smoke and never getting a word in edgeways."

We turned into the narrow road where I had walked yesterday. Soon we were passing by the long wire-netting fence where the deer were. They were a little nearer to us this time, so that even in the half-light we could see them clearly. John stood up in his stirrups to get a good look. When he settled back in the saddle, he surprised me by saying, "I'd love to own a dozen of them. They're the queerest animals I ever saw in my life."

"Colman Donnelly said the same—that he'd like to own a few," I said.

Now I remembered that Colman had not been at Patsy's place this evening. He would be sorry to miss the news, I thought, since he was so much interested in everything concerning the deer. Uncomfortably I remembered too how he had said he still felt he had rights to the land, though he had sold it to Michael Joyce. I let all thought of him trickle away then, not wanting to spoil our present journey.

The wire fence continued for a long way and then made a turn to the right. I could see that it enclosed a huge piece of the hillside. Our road went straight on, dropping first into a desolate valley with bog holes shining black in the dim evening light and gray-green bogland as far as we could see. Then we mounted again, between bare rocks which had patches of grass here and there on them and sloping tracts of land covered with heather and furze. Sheep were grazed there, John told me, and I wondered how my cousin from Roscommon would feel if he had this kind of land. His sheep had huge green fields to graze, and he had told me that this was the only sensible way to raise sheep. I could still hear the contempt in his voice when he spoke of the mountainy sheep of Connemara.

All at once I remembered that I had not written to my mother after all. I would do so the moment we would get back, I thought, and I hoped it would not be too late.

As we went over the mountain, night fell. The moonlight was surprisingly strong. We could see the road quite clearly, and the landscape on either side of us, almost as bright as day. We could feel that the horses did not like traveling by night.

Their ears twitched nervously and their eyes rolled, and now and then they danced aside to avoid a quivering shadow at their feet.

High up on the mountain we stopped at a place where a roadside stream widened, so that they could drink. We did not dismount, but let them bend their long necks down to suck up the water while we leaned back in the saddles. At last they lifted their heads, almost at the same moment, shook the water off their whiskers, and we started off again. This time they seemed more contented. We trotted them up the hills and walked them down. They moved always shoulder to shoulder, as if they liked each other's company. John's horse was a chestnut, as slim as Canyon's, almost as if he had Arab blood in him too. His shoulders were as narrow and his head as small, and his little round hoofs were as neat as any Connemara pony I had ever seen.

"He has won five races," John said, stroking the horse's neck so that he shook his head until his mane danced. "I'll race him this summer myself, if Tim will let me. Tim has always raced him until now and he doesn't want to give him up. But it would only be for one race, till I'd see how I'd get on. Maybe you'll still be here. Maybe Canyon would let you race that one of his. Canyon is too old for it himself. You could ask him when we get back."

"When will these races be?"

"There's some in July and some in August."

"I could ask," I said, but I did not dare to think of where I would be or what I would be doing in July and August. Long before that, I might be sneaking along under the ditches on my way back to Galway, with the men of Connemara on my track.

John was saying, "We have the races on the big strands at low tide—Omey strand is the best of them. Man, it's a great sight! You can't go home until you've seen Omey races. The tinkers come with stalls, selling oranges and apples and sweets and biscuits. The whole of west Connacht will be there."

And I might see the Burkes, I thought. Surely they would not miss such a chance of picking pockets. I could feel myself go rigid with rage at the memory of what they had done to me, and I longed for the moment when I would see them again, to pay them back for it. I did not know then how soon I was going to have my wish.

After a while we fell silent. The mountain was so desolate, with no sign of a house of any kind, that it depressed us in spite of ourselves. A little wind nipped at us, a mean wind that was weak, but that still whined against the rocky outcroppings as we passed them by. Curlews whistled with a lonesome sound, far away but clear, and gave us an unpleasant feeling of isolation in that vast space. We saw several foxes, prowling on their night's business. They were not very shy of us. They stood still to watch us pass, with their ears cocked and the moonlight gleaming on their white chests. Afterward, as we rode on, we heard their oddly cheerful bark, high and light.

At last it seemed that the valleys looked a little less dreary and the hills less stark. Real grass grew by the roadside instead of the sedge and heather we had seen until now. We passed a few cows, and a thatched house all shut up and dark. I wondered what the people would think if they woke in the night and heard our horses' hoofs passing by. Perhaps they were used to it. Perhaps they had heard Patsy Carroll and Morgan Curran a few days ago, and the soft patter of the deer's hoofs with the horses. Perhaps they were the kind of people who don't ask questions about such things, not even of each other. I knew that I would not have liked to live at the edge of that great waste of mountain.

The moon still gave plenty of light, though it was not as strong as it had been earlier. Our road passed between banks with hedges of thorn growing on top—the first I had seen since I had left Galway town. This was a very different kind of land. The stone walls and the rocky fields by the seacoast might have belonged to another country.

Then we saw the lake. We halted our horses to gaze at it from the top of a hill. It shone slate-gray in the moonlight, patched here and there with black where the islands were. I was surprised at the irregularity of its banks. Everywhere there were promontories reaching far out into the lake, sometimes seeming almost to touch the islands. The islands themselves were all shapes—some long and narrow, some small and round, some rising to little peaks with trees growing on top, as we could see by their softer lines even at this distance. The far shore seemed rather flat, but at our side of the lake there were hills like the one where we stood.

John yawned and said, "The night is half over. We'll go down to the lake and pitch the tent, and have a fine sleep before we do anything useful."

The thought of sleep was sweet to me, you may be sure. We were stiff from sitting in the saddle and we had not wanted to dismount and limber up for fear of losing time. Our only rest had been when we had stopped to let the horses drink from the streams which seemed to follow the road no matter where it went. I thought with respect of Patsy Carroll, who had traveled this road twice over in one night.

The horses were tired too. Their hoofs were rolling on the gravel road so that we did not dare to hurry them. Then the road became smoother and less precipitous, and they broke into a trot of their own accord as if they knew the end of the journey was near.

A mile from the shore of the lake, we came to a comfortable village with neat houses, well thatched and hedged around with yews. I remembered Patsy's contemptuous statement that this was hungry country. It did not look hungry to me, but perhaps he had found that the people were not as hospitable as they were by the sea. Passing through the village, we kept to the thick grass by the side of the road, so that we made hardly a sound.

John seemed to know exactly where we were going. He led the way along a grassy track from the road to the shore of the lake. It was a little bay, with a beach of fine gravel in the middle and tall rushes at either side. There was a wide stretch of soft, fine grass above the beach, sloping gently upward to a thin wood that looked like ash, its leaves were so feathery. A clump of hazel bushes grew toward the end of the beach, and John rode straight for this and around to the other side of it.

"We'll put up the tent here," he said. "If anyone takes a quick look this way, they won't see it. We'll tether the horses in among the trees. But this is a quiet place. There's no one will come here until we've finished our business."

"Where are the deer?"

"That's Inish Goill out there." He pointed toward the end of one of the arms of the little bay. "We'll need the daylight to see it."

We slid to the ground and loosened our packs so that they fell in a heap. Then we led the horses slowly in among the trees. They were ash trees, all right. Their trunks were thin and tall. We unsaddled the horses and tethered them a little distance apart. Then John took out his knife and cut a strong stick for himself.

"There's nothing I like better than an ashplant," he said.

Grass grew in the wood, and the horses began to crop it at once. I felt at home in this place, because it was so like our own lake. The little sounds pleased me—the tiny wash of the water at the edge of the lake when it stirred the dead pieces of reed that lay there; the rustle of the reeds that grew tall at either end of the little bay; the faint, roaring sound of the wind in distant pine trees; the night calls of various waterfowl. The smells were delightful too—mild scents of grass and pines carried on the damp air, very different from the wild smell of salt and rotting seaweed that I had experienced for the last few days.

We got the tent up quickly. The sound of the mallet on the pegs seemed to thunder through the air for miles. The pegs went easily into the soft ground, so that two or three blows were enough for each. Soon we were inside, munching Sarah John's bread as we lay slackly on the ground.

John gave a little chuckle and said, "Now I have my wish. There's no place in the wide world where I'd rather be than where I am now."

A minute later I could tell by his gentle, even breathing that he had fallen asleep.

# ≥ 8

I WAS DEADLY TIRED, AND yet an hour passed and I could not fall asleep as John had done. My ears seemed stretched to catch strange sounds, creakings and whisperings, that were carried on the quiet air along with the rustle of the water on the shore. My eyes were wide open, as if this would help me to hear better. I began to try recognizing the calls of the birds that I knew —coots and herons and waterhens, and the soft whistle of a curlew. I heard one of the horses move suddenly, and this was such an everyday sound that it was a comfort. It was odd, I thought, that I was so uneasy tonight though I had company for the first time in my tent. I began to doze, deliberately shutting my eyes and relaxing my tired muscles.

Suddenly I was wide awake again, with all my senses horribly alert. Something was moving out there. I listened for a moment and then I shook John's shoulder very gently. He made no sound, but I knew he was awake. I felt his hand go down to grasp the ashplant that he had laid beside him when he went to sleep.

Very quietly I began to crawl out of my sleeping bag. John was freer than I was, since he was only wrapped around in two blankets, lying on an old oilskin of Patsy's. We did not need to speak nor see each other. Like a shadow, he rolled over to untie the flap of the tent. A moment later, the fabric of the tent sagged a little at the closed end, as a peg was pulled out.

"It's the Burkes!" I yelled at the top of my voice.

John heaved himself out of the tent and darted around to the end of it. I was only a second behind him. I heard him lash out with his stick and strike twice at someone who howled like a dog. The moonlight was too faint to show us his face. All we could see was a thin, ragged figure that sprang away like a goat. John went after him and aimed another blow at him, but the man dodged to one side at the right moment so that it missed. The same happened when I threw myself on him. One second before I would have had him by the legs, he was off with a sideways spring and I was rolling uselessly on the ground. Then we saw him fly across the grass at an astonishing speed, almost without a sound, and disappear among the trees. Again the horses moved.

"I know him." My breath was gone and I could hardly speak. "The Burkes. Tinkers. I'd know him anywhere. He stole my money. He took the tent from over my head. The east side of Galway. He's as quiet as a rat."

"As an eel," said John. "I got two good whacks in on him, anyway, that he won't forget for a while. What was he doing?"

"After the tent, I suppose. I tell you he took the tent from over me once and I never felt him at it. It was his own tent that time. He was making off with my money. There must have been a few of the children or maybe his wife here with him tonight to hold it, so that it wouldn't fall on our faces when he pulled out the pegs. That's how he does it."

"But surely we would have felt him and heard him. Surely he couldn't do it so quietly that it wouldn't wake us up."

"He did it to me before, I tell you," I said irritably. "I woke in the morning and the tent was gone. I suppose I'm a good sleeper."

"You must be, indeed."

"Did you see anyone with him?"

"Children, I think. They were gone in a flash. Well, there's no doubt but he has the neck of Old Nick," said John, almost with admiration.

I was furious that he had got away. Yet I could imagine that if we had got him down and had seemed to be getting the better of him, a swarm of children would have shot out of cover and attacked us from the back. Two of us would not be likely to be a match for the whole family. For all we knew, at this moment they could all be watching us from the wood, like rabbits ready to pop into their burrows. I was tempted to call out threats into the darkness but some good sense prevented me.

We inspected the tent and found that two of the pegs had been pulled out and a stone laid on the guy rope to hold it in place temporarily. It seemed likely that Burke's intention had been to do the same with all the pegs and then to lift the tent off us quietly and sneak away with it, or else to snatch it suddenly and make a run for it. Our surprise would have given him the time he would need to get away. At night in the trees, it would be impossible to catch up with him. I shivered suddenly.

John said, "We might as well go to bed. He won't come back tonight, if I know his kind."

But we could not lie down quietly as if nothing had happened. We tried it, and found ourselves leaping up every moment to listen for sounds of the Burkes' return. After a while I got uneasy about the horses and we had to go and see that they were safe. It was not pleasant to go in among the dark trees, with a feeling that a whole family of Burkes might be hiding there. Nothing rustled, there was no sound of scuttling feet, however, and we found the horses lying quietly at their ease. They would not have been so if strange hands had been attempting to lead them away.

"Tinkers never steal good horses," John said. "They only take the ones that no one seems to care about, or ones that are left a long time out on grass, that won't be missed for a while. And they heard you name them, unless they're deaf. They know that if our horses disappeared, we'd have the Guards after their tails in two shakes."

The dawn was breaking when we got back to the tent. We did not go inside, but went down to the edge of the lake to watch the faint light grow, seeming to come up out of the water itself. The trees were full of a whitish mist that disappeared gradually as we watched. A waterhen paddled speedily along by one of the arms of the little bay. We could see her busy little head bobbing earnestly up and down.

"There's Inish Goill," said John, pointing. "Now you can see how close it is to the shore. You would nearly think it's not an island at all, but there's a little channel of water between it and the mainland." He stopped suddenly and craned his head to peer into the mist. Then he gave a short laugh. "Do you see the smoke? There's someone at home."

"Is there a house there?" I asked, surprised.

In any talk of it I had heard, no one had mentioned a family living on the island. Now that I could see it clearly, it looked a good island to me, with plenty of fine trees and some pasture. If it had been on our lake at home, someone would have made good use of it.

John said, "Not a family, exactly. We'll get our breakfast, though, if I'm not mistaken. I could eat the side of a house this minute."

The thought of breakfast made me hurry after him. I was desperately hungry, and only a moment before I had been wishing we had brought a whole loaf of bread with us, instead of the scraps that we had eaten at the end of our long ride. I could see the smoke—a thin, straight line of gray against the misty trees—but I could not see a chimney.

At the western side of the little bay, we walked out to the end of the promontory. Ash and rowan trees grew here, and brambles and ivy covered the ground. A faint path showed, where these had been trodden flat and had only partly sprung back again. We followed this to the tip, where a sort of causeway had been built out into the lake. It was of rough stone, blackened and pitted by the water over many years. It had been widened at the end and three long planks had been laid there to join a similar causeway that stretched toward it from the island, making an uneasy bridge.

John was waiting for me. "Quiet as a mouse now," he warned.

We crossed to the island by the planks, without a sound. It was like walking a tightrope, balancing carefully with every step so that the planks would not roll and clatter.

On the island, John moved even more cautiously and slowly, stopping to listen and placing his feet with exactness on the soft pine needles. I kept as close behind him as I could, and I was at his shoulder when we came to the edge of a little grassy clearing where three men were sitting over a little fire of sticks. A blackened tin can hung over the fire on an improvised tripod of long sticks. The smoke rose straight into the quiet air. The wood was dry and it blazed up well. One of the men continually fed the fire from a little pile of chips that he had collected beside him.

John said, "Good day to you all."

Two of the men sprang to their knees at once. The man who was tending the fire gave a half-roll over onto one elbow. Then they all relaxed and settled back as they had been. One of them, a short, fat man with a tweed cap, said in an aggrieved tone, "You frightened the heart in us. Why did you sneak up like that?"

"You know well why," said John easily. "If we had made a noise, we'd never see you at all."

"True for you," said another man, who had a very soft voice, as if he were always telling a great secret. "We'd have scattered like rabbits."

The third man had an air of being rather above such exaggerations. He went on with tending the fire, lifting his eyebrows and turning down the corners of his mouth to show his disagreement. After a moment he asked, "Are there any more of ye there?"

131 ✍

"No. Just the two of us."

"Where did ye spring from?"

"We rode over from Cois Fhairrge."

This name I knew was used to describe miles and miles of the country west of Galway, and it meant simply the seacoast.

"Ah." He threw a handful of tiny chips on the fire, making it blaze up suddenly. "I can guess why you're here. Did you see anyone about this part of the world?"

"A tinker, a short while ago. A whole bunch of them, indeed. I think they're the Burkes."

"How long ago?"

"A couple of hours. It was dark."

"Then how did you know it was the Burkes?"

"By the go of them," said John calmly.

"You weren't talking to them?"

"No."

"Were they on their way here?" the man with the cap asked eagerly. "We're waiting all night for them, to mend the still."

The fire man threw him a furious look. John said, as if he had noticed nothing, "Maybe we put them off. Maybe they were afraid to come over when they knew we were about here. We had no speech with them."

The soft-voiced man said, "Let ye sit down a while anyway and eat a bite with us. That water should be boiled soon."

We moved forward. The grass was wet with dew, but they had each brought a stone to sit on. We did not fancy this and instead we stayed a little apart, where the dry pine needles covered the ground softly. Steam was rising from the can now and the water was singing. The short man in the cap took a tightly wrapped packet of tea out of his pocket and emptied it into the can. Then he got up and went off among the trees for a minute and came back with an old flour sack swinging in one hand. This contained two loaves of soda-bread, ready cut and buttered, half a dozen hard-boiled eggs, and a whiskey bottle full of milk. We drank the tea, foul-tasting and the color of bog water, in turns from two chipped mugs which were passed

133

from hand to hand. The fire man became a little more friendly when he had eaten.

"The Burkes are very easily frightened," he said, "And they're not easy to find. We weren't even sure they had our message, but they must have had, for nothing else would bring them here."

"They're good tradesmen?"

"The best in Ireland. The father is a master hand and the eldest boy is taking after him. The second one is shaping the same way. A fine, useful family. They can make and mend."

"A strange thing about them is that they never owned a caravan," said the short man. "They could easily afford it, with all the money they make one way and another."

"I know why it is," said the soft-spoken man. "They like to be independent, that's why. They can move faster and quieter, with a tent only, and no one takes any notice of them."

Suddenly I feared for my tent again, and for our two horses. I whispered to John, "Maybe when we go ashore we'll find they have made off with our things after all."

"The horses—" For a moment he looked alarmed, though he had told me the tinkers would not touch them. Just then we heard swift steps approaching from the wood. They were not cautious as ours had been, though they were naturally light. Our three companions looked at each other with satisfaction.

The fire man said, "Here they are. There's no one else walks like that."

Sure enough, with his strange, prancing step the father of the Burkes was coming toward us. Behind him came two boys aged about twelve and fourteen. They were small like their father, and they had already begun to walk like him. They looked quickly around the group. They all had sharp brown eyes which shone like glass marbles in their sun-browned faces.

The short man said, "Ye're welcome, at last. We're waiting all night for ye."

"We got held up with some other business," said Burke with

a long expressionless look at us. "You know we never can say for sure when we'll come."

"Better late than never," said the fire man. "Had you a bite to eat?"

"No, then. We'd be glad of it."

They ate the bread like animals, falling on it for a sudden bite and clutching it between times in their closed hands as if they expected to have to defend it. As I watched them, it occurred to me that it would never be possible to vanquish them. The most we could hope for was that they would develop respect for our power to defend our property, and so leave us alone. I had certainly never expected to sit again in apparent friendship by a fire with them. When they had finished eating, they sat quietly and waited.

The short man said, "Well, come and look at the still. There's no time to waste. Did you pull the planks over after you?"

"Of course. We're not fond of visitors either." Again he looked directly at us.

The fire man said, "They're not visitors. They're here on business too."

He scattered his fire and stamped out the smouldering edges of the pieces of wood. The men seemed to take it for granted that we would follow them. Still, we kept very quiet in case we would be told to go about our business and leave them to theirs. No one said anything. In single file, with the short man leading, we went among the pine trees until we came to a small hollow. It was round, so regularly shaped that I think it was man-made, but that must have been a long time before because now it was covered with grass. The pines grew tall all around it. In the middle, resting on a hearth of flat stones, was the poteen still.

I had never seen one before, though I knew they were to be found here and there in my part of the country too. Making poteen was a very secret business, as all law breaking must be.

135

It was necessary, some people said, since the whiskey you bought in shops was much too dear, and guests at a wedding or a wake must be treated with proper hospitality all the same. A great many people said it was wrong, and would have nothing to do with it, but they would not help the Guards to find the stills nor inform on their owners either.

The still was about four feet high as far as the shoulders, shaped rather like a milk churn but much wider. A spiral of copper piping—the "worm"—came out of the top of it. When it was in use, some sort of condenser must have been fitted over it, but this was not visible now.

The still was of tin, riveted together with a kind of workmanship which showed it had been made by tinkers. If it were to last, it should have been made of galvanized iron. However, this would have been too heavy to transport, and in any case the tinkers did not normally use this material. A great patch of rust showed on the side.

"It's full of pin holes," the short man said, and he kicked at the rusty patch. "You'll have to cut that piece out and put in a patch."

"You should have covered it," said Burke. "Of course it rusted, out in the open like that."

"We did cover it," said the short man, "but the rust got at it all the same. It's a crime to have to keep it outside. We're thinking of putting up a little wooden hut to house it."

"That would keep it, surely."

One of the boys had a bundle of tools in an oilskin, and some sheets of shiny, crackling tin. They went to work at once on the still, while the three men stood by, watching them.

After a moment, John said, "We'll be off. Thanks for the breakfast."

"You're welcome," they said absently, never taking their eyes off the tinkers.

Silently we left them. John seemed to know the island well. He led the way through the pines for several hundred yards, until they came to an end and we were looking downhill at a wide green pasture that ran down to the water's edge. The broad lake stretched away and away in front of us, with the islands here and there, that we had seen from the hilltop. It was clear, bright daylight now and the water was quite calm and smooth.

"There they are," John said, "all together."

The little group of deer stood not far off at the edge of the wood. While we watched, they began to move away from us, browsing as they went on the blackberry bushes and thick weeds that grew there. I could see the buck's tall, branching horns, much bigger and wider spread than the does'.

John said, "They look very contented, I must say. We couldn't have picked a better place. No one ever comes here except the men that make the poteen, and they're not likely to give away anyone's secrets for fear of what might happen to themselves."

It was easy to see the sense of that. I said, "But who owns the island? There's fine grazing going to waste on it."

"It belongs to a woman in England whose father and all before him were landlords around here," John said. "But her big house is in ruins and she hasn't set foot in Ireland for more than forty years, I've heard. They never made use of the island anyway, except to look at it, and that from a distance."

And they probably never knew that the offshore side of it was being used for grazing by their neighbors, I thought, nor that poteen was being made in the hollow.

We walked down to the shore. I wished there were a boat there—a calm, decent boat made of wood, with wide-bladed oars that would send you gliding along on the still water, where never a shark nor any other form of sea monster would dare to show his nose. It amazed me now to think that only a few days before I had leaned out of a crazy canvas boat on a heaving sea and stabbed a shark with a billhook.

John was watching me. "It's a different story from our part of the world," he said. "And still I think I'd like it fine, when I'd get used to it."

I began to tell him about trout fishing on a warm summer evening, when the little fat fish rose one after the other and you took home just what you needed. You sent your boat drifting along so gently that the trout took no notice of you, but continued to jump after flies on the surface of the water, making eddies and ripples that widened until they became invisible.

"Our lake hasn't as many islands as this," I said, "but it has enough for us—"

Then I remembered that I was to have been a city boy, from Sligo town, who knew little or nothing about country ways. I had not thought of this for several days. John seemed not to have noticed anything. He picked up a stone and sent it spinning over the surface of the water. It hopped along, six or seven times.

"It's not often we get a sea smooth enough for this game," he said with satisfaction, picking up another stone.

But as he stood up, we both saw a movement at the edge of the trees. A moment later Colman Donnelly stepped out of cover and began to walk toward us.

"Now in the name of all that's wonderful," said John softly, "what's bringing him here? It can't be a message, because no one in their right senses would send that little pysawn on a message. Patsy told me they didn't even tell him that the deer are here, for they wouldn't trust him that far."

"Then how did they come to leave them on his land before bringing them here?"

"They were on land that he owns over by Screeb," said John. "No one else has a second quarter so handy, miles from his own house."

He said this with a kind of contempt, as if there were some disgrace in being so well off. I wondered how much harm I had done, in revealing to Colman where the deer were now. Remembering back, I knew that I should have noticed the men avoiding mention of the island's name while he was there. Even now I could not see that there was any harm in his knowing, as it seemed clear that removing the deer was only to be used as a sign of strength and solidarity against Michael Joyce. I remembered uncomfortably how Colman had invited me to his house, through a desire for my company, I had imagined. I had thought he was lonely, but now I saw it was more likely that he was ingratiating himself with me in the hope of picking my brains, such as they were.

Colman was smiling as he came through the grass toward us. We could see that he was trying to please, but there was a cold look in his eyes which he could not conceal and which gave him away at once. It may have been this that the men saw, and that made them distrust him. They would have understood his bitterness against Michael Joyce, though it was not very sensible, and they would have forgiven it because it was not directed against themselves. But his present expression was that of a man who was at war with the whole world, I thought.

"I saw your horses in the wood," he said when he was close enough. "I tied mine with them."

"What brought you?" John asked abruptly.

"Curiosity. It's a long ride alone. I would have been glad of your company, if I had known you were on the same road."

We made no reply to this. Colman went on, "I saw three tinkers coming onto the island, very soon after I got here myself. I hid myself from them, in the bushes. They did a strange thing. They pulled the bridge over after themselves. If I had been a bit later, I wouldn't have got onto the island at all. Now I wonder what they're doing here, so early in the morning and so secretly."

"They're mending a still," John said shortly.

"Ah. I'm glad to know that." He glanced toward the deer. "You came to look at the deer, I suppose."

"Yes."

"They look fine."

"They do."

"Fine and healthy."

"Yes."

"I'd like to get closer to them. They're not fond of company."

He looked toward the little group of deer, and I saw the same longing expression on his face that he had had when he had told me that he would like to keep a few deer himself. He was a bit late with his enthusiasm for farming, I thought. If he had been more energetic when he was younger, he might still be the owner of his fine house and farm, and he would have saved his neighbors all their present ill temper.

"When are you thinking of going home?" Colman asked.

"We're not expected until tomorrow," John said. He seemed to make an effort to be more civil as he went on: "We'll go back by a different road, that will land us down at Carraroe."

"Very nice. And Peter will see a bit more of the country. I'll come with you."

"You're welcome."

I admired John for the ungrudging way that he said this, like a woman who welcomes the village bore to sit by her fire, makes her a cup of tea, and asks after her health as anxiously as if she were her dearest friend. I wondered if I would ever achieve this polite patience myself. It seemed very unlikely then, but it did come at last, with time and practice.

Colman said, "What are you doing with the deer?"

"Nothing," John said. "Just seeing they're safe and well. If the planks were left there long, the deer might wander off all over Connacht and never be seen again."

Colman's face brightened at this. " 'Tis true for you. That might happen easily," he said. "They'd never be found again if they got off onto the mountains." He gave his odd laugh. "The next we'd hear there would be a huge herd of wild deer in Connemara, like there used to be in ancient times." After a pause he added, "Ye won't be going today, so?"

"That's right."

"How will ye spend the day? Here on the island?"

"Maybe. What about yourself?" John asked.

"I have a few friends around these parts," said Colman. "I'll pay them a visit, and then I'll come back in the evening to see if ye're ready to travel. But I'm thinking ye'd need to sleep tonight. If ye're going back by Carraroe, surely there's no need to travel by night. If you started off this minute, ye could be home and dried by the evening."

"We're not expected till tomorrow," John said firmly. "We'll go to bed early and start off at the dawn of the morning. Where will you sleep?"

"My friends will let me have the settle," said Colman.

You may be sure I was glad to hear this. I had no wish to have him spend the night in my little tent, but of course I should have had to make the offer rather than leave him out under the sky.

On our way back to the bridge, we kept well away from the hollow where the still was. I would have liked to see it again, but Colman stayed closely with us, almost as if he were herding us along. He used an irritating, forgiving tone to us, as some people do to boys, as if no matter what his own foolishness, he was still bound to be wiser than us. He helped us to replace the planks, and crossing the bridge, he even put his hand on my arm, as if I would be likely to fall off without his guidance.

The horses whinnied when they saw us.

"We'll take them away and give them a feed of oats," John said. "And they could do with a bit of exercise."

Colman had not bothered to unsaddle his horse. It was a depressed-looking bay, that might have been handsome if it ever had a good grooming. I remembered how Colman had said that deer look after themselves, and I guessed that he would grudge the time he should have spent in looking after his horse.

Our saddles were safe, lying where we had left them on the grass. I guessed that they must have been a sore temptation to the Burkes and that only the fact that I had yelled out their name in the night had saved our property. Before mounting, I peeped into the tent and saw that everything was just as we had left it.

In single file we rode away from the lake shore, John and I going in front and Colman following us. Out on the road, where it forked north and south, John said, pointing away from the village we had passed last night, "We'll be going this way. There's a good shop in Ballinahown where they'll have whatever we need for ourselves and the horses. We'll see you at six o'clock in the morning. Good day to you."

"Good day to you," said Colman.

He sat half-turned in the saddle and watched us ride off.

"What about the plank bridge? The deer could walk off the island now and no one to stop them."

"They would be stopped," said John. "You may be sure that a Burke child was following us around the island, and by now he's sitting in the bushes guarding the bridge so that nothing will come on or off."

This meant that we were free to enjoy ourselves, and the unexpectedness of the holiday made it all the more pleasant.

On our right hand, as we rode along, we could see the glitter of the lake beyond the fields and woods. It was a fine, sunny day but a wind had sprung up, which became a little stronger during the morning. It made us hungry, so that when we reached the village of Ballinahown after an hour's ride, we went straight to the shop and bought some buns.

It was a fine wide shop with a long counter across the back. The counter was piled high with coils of rope, lanterns, pots and pans, bales of knitting wool, socks, boxes of shirts, and a glass case of bread and buns. Through a gap in the middle, the owner did his business of selling. He was a smooth, comfortable-looking man with a round bald head like a baby and a soft, apologetic voice.

"Ah, yes, the horses, the horses," he said when we asked for some oats. "And they can do with a drop of water, but not at the same time as the oats, of course. Never give a horse oats and water at the same time or he'll swell up and burst. Did you know that?"

We said that we did, and agreed that it was a necessary piece of knowledge for anyone who had to do with horses. When we had fed them, we bought some potatoes and sausages, which were by now the only things I could think of eating out of doors. Then we climbed wearily onto the horses again and started back to our camping ground.

# 9

IT WAS WELL AFTER NOON when we got back to the shore of the lake. There was a high, hot sun. Flies buzzed all around us—big, healthy, iridescent flies that seemed to think we had come specially to keep them company. We lit a fire of sticks which made them keep at a civil distance, and when the fire glowed, we cooked our sausages over it. John admired my little stove, on which we boiled the potatoes, but I would have liked a second fire of sticks for that. He laughed at me.

"Why not?" I said. "If you had a long enough hearth, you could have three or four fires on it and a pot boiling on every one of them."

The wood smoke gave a delightful flavor to the sausages. Cooking and eating them kept us awake, but afterward we sat in the sun feeling dazed. I longed to crawl into the tent and sleep, but John would not agree.

"We'll have to stay awake at least until the men get off the island," he said, "and until we see the bridge taken down. That's what we came for."

He gave a long yawn. I felt my jaws open wide in sympathy. We tried swimming in the lake, but afterward we found that unless we repeated the exercise we were more sleepy than ever. We walked about, and took the horses down to water them, and collected sticks for the fire, and at last went onto the island again to see how the men were faring.

They were sitting in a ring eating bread and more hard-boiled eggs when we arrived. They looked very tired. Like ourselves, they had lost a night's sleep. The Burkes were alert and lively as ever. The father turned expressionless, shining eyes on us when we appeared and did not join in the greeting that the others gave us.

"All finished?" John asked.

"Yes, and a lovely job," said the short man. "It's like new."

"Can we go and look at it?"

"Surely."

We went through the woods to the hollow and there was the still, with a huge patch, almost halfway around its body, of shining tin. The patch was made up of several square pieces, riveted together.

"They're experts, all right," said John in admiration. "It's a big job. No wonder it took them so long to finish it."

We went to look at the deer and found them at the water's edge, drinking. The sun was still high, a dazzling light that bored into me horribly so that I could no longer care for anything except to get away from it into cool darkness. Like sleepwalkers, we went back to the bridge, and found the men there waiting for us. The Burkes had already gone ashore. They stood in a line and watched while we all crossed, after which the men lifted the planks one by one and carried them to their hiding place in a tall, thick thornbush that grew a little distance beyond the narrow channel. Then they all set off together in the direction of the village.

"It's not milk they're after, by the look of them," said John. "I wonder if they'll meet Colman."

We went back and sat in front of the tent, unable to speak, barely succeeding in staying awake, until the sun had gone down behind the mountain to the west of us. Gradually the sky darkened and the treetops stood out sharp like teeth against the light. When a little mist had begun to dim the outlines of

145 ✍

the island and the trees, with hardly a word we crawled into
the tent and lay down. I can never forget the sensation of that
falling asleep. It was a real falling, like letting go of a rope and
sliding slowly and gently into a delightful softness which
wrapped me around completely.

We would have slept far into the next day if Colman had not
kept his appointment with us. It was a sharp, clear morning
with high, windy clouds. The grass was heavy with dew, already steaming gently in the sun. The lake water was ruffled to

a dark gray-blue, and we could hear that strange, even, roaring sound that the wind makes in the tops of pine trees, and that reminded me so sharply of home.

Colman had brought milk for our tea, and some bread. His horse was rambling about, grazing, with the reins trailing loose. Colman looked very tired, and I began to wonder if the explanation of his laziness might be that he was not very healthy. I could not imagine his ever plunging into the lake for a quick swim before breakfast, as we did now.

"Ye slept well," he said. "It took me a good five minutes to wake ye up."

"I could sleep all day," John said.

"Did ye hear any noise in the night?" Colman asked. "Did anyone come poking around?"

"Not a soul," I said. "And if they did, we wouldn't have heard them. If it had been last night the Burkes came for the tent, they would have got away with it easily."

"The Burkes?"

"Those tinkers you saw yesterday. They came the first night and tried to take the tent from over our heads. It's a trick they're good at, but we caught them."

"You frightened them off?"

"We did. They were afraid to come back. John left a mark on one of them that he won't forget in a hurry."

We entertained ourselves at breakfast with some more boasting of the same kind, which I squirmed to remember afterward. When we had finished eating, we packed up the tent and the rest of our gear. Colman was fidgeting around impatiently.

"We'd better get on the road quickly. We have a long way to go," he said. "What's keeping you?"

"We'll be ready in a few minutes," John said. "We must see the deer once more and then we can be off."

"The deer? Why should you see the deer?"

"That's what we came for," John said mildly.

"But you saw them yesterday."

"True enough. We saw them twice and we'll see them again today."

"There's no sense to that."

"If you like, Colman, you can be off on your own," John said. "We wouldn't like to be keeping you as you're in such a hurry. We have all day if we want it, but I suppose you want to get home early."

To my great surprise Colman agreed to this. He did not seem to have noticed the incivility of the suggestion. He had promised his wife, he said, and he was not as young as he used to be, so he might have to rest a few times on the way. And he called to his horse, which waited for him obediently, climbed into the saddle, and set off without a word of farewell. We looked after him in astonishment.

"Good riddance to bad rubbish," John said after a moment. "I wonder what came over him. Yesterday he was saying he'd enjoy our company on the road back and today he wouldn't even wait half an hour for us."

"We're in luck," I said. "I don't like an inch of him. The road back will be a lot shorter without him."

But afterward, while we were laying the planks across to the island, I said, "It's a pity Colman went off in such a hurry. He'd be useful now, if we had him."

"He'd probably just stand by and give instructions," John said. "Did you notice his hands—how soft they are? He'd be afraid of hurting himself."

The planks were very hard to manage. We laid only two of them, pushing them close together as best we could. Then we skipped across onto the island. We walked along the little stone causeway. At the base of it, John said, "The deer have been here. Look at their tracks."

Sure enough, the soft ground under the pine trees was pitted with little hoof marks, rather as if some sheep had been there. We followed the tracks around by the shore of the island until we came to the grassy pasture where we had seen the deer yesterday. There was no sign of them now. We skirted the edge of the woods, peering in among the trees where they might have lain hidden in the long grass and brambles. We went in there, shouting and clapping our hands to send them galloping out into the open. We went through the hollow where the still was, and to the clearing where the poteen men had had their fire, and so around to the causeway and the bridge again.

Then John said in despair, "Those deer are gone. You can feel it in the air."

I said that this could not be true, not wanting to believe him. We went over the island again, yard by yard, keeping a little distance apart so that we would be sure not to miss the deer in some quiet place where they might be lying. But it was a small island, and at last we knew that we had covered the whole of it, and that what John had said was true. The deer were gone.

"The Burkes," I said bitterly. "They're thieves by nature. They couldn't keep their hands off those deer, though they won't be able to keep them, nor to sell them either."

John's teeth were clenched in rage. He walked up and down on the soft pine needles, kicking them into the air in little puffs with sheer temper.

"Why did we sleep?" he demanded. "Why did we let them get away with it? We should have sat up all night and watched—"

"We might have gone home last night," I reminded him, "if we hadn't been so tired after the first night."

"That's true, I suppose. Colman advised us to go, but I wanted to spend another night in the little tent. How can we go home and say they're gone?"

But there was nothing else to be done, as we realized when we had talked it over. In the vast spaces of Connemara, hundreds of square miles, we could search forever and not find the deer. We could not ask questions, since these would reveal that we knew the deer had been on the island. We would be blamed forever after if we were to draw attention in any way to Inish Goill.

"It would be fine if we could ask that shopkeeper in Ballinahown," John said. "I'd say it would be hard to do anything in this part of the world that he wouldn't get to know of it. Anyone that has a shop hears everything. And he looks like a man that doesn't have too much to say. Did you notice he didn't ask us any questions yesterday?"

"It's true," I said. "He seemed to have no curiosity about us at all."

"And how could you trust a man like that?" John said. "It's not natural. It could be that he would give his word to us and afterward whisper it all to someone else. That's what he is, I'm sure—a whisperer."

"Colman wanted us to go away," I said. "Maybe he's at the back of this. He covets those deer. He almost told me so. Yesterday he seemed very much interested in the idea that they might wander off to the mountains and breed wild. Maybe he was thinking that if that happened, he would be able to help himself to a few and keep them. But it would be a chancy business. Much better and surer to get the Burkes to steal them for him and hide them somewhere."

"Where?"

"At his place in Screeb."

"If they're in Screeb, they'll be easy to find. We'll go home that way." After a pause, he said, "But Colman didn't seem to know the Burkes."

"Maybe he didn't know their name, or maybe he was just letting on not to know them. He certainly didn't want us to come here this morning for a last look at the deer."

"That's true," John said. "This morning he was nervous. I was wondering if those friends with the settle bed were all that glad to see him."

We looked for tracks of the deer on the mainland shore, but we found nothing. The grass was too thick there, and they must have been herded into it at once. Only if they had walked on the little sandy strip by the water's edge would they have left hoofprints.

Silently we saddled the horses and mounted, each with a

pack in front. In single file, we rode out onto the shore. From our elevated position we looked away off toward the hills, which were dappled with sunlight and differently colored vegetation. A herd of deer would be quite invisible against that background. Their gentle, slow movements would be masked by the grass and the bushes swaying in the wind. Their mottled skins would be indistinguishable from the natural colors all around them.

I was glad that John did not speak for a while. I was thinking about Michael Joyce and what I would tell him when I would meet him next. He seemed to me, now, to be farther away than ever from getting back his deer and living in peace with his neighbors. This time, I wondered, would he have patience again, or would he think the time had come to call in the Guards? It would be my business to persuade him that this would be useless. I could imagine the Guards blundering through Connemara, asking questions about a herd of deer and getting nothing in reply except a series of solemn yarns that they would not even be expected to believe. They and Michael Joyce could only end by being made to look mighty foolish.

The road to Screeb took us north for several miles, until we turned to the left at Maam Cross. Now suddenly we left the comfortable country of trees and hedges and well-kept farmhouses behind, and found ourselves in a long green valley through which the road seemed to wind endlessly. The west wind swept toward us with a whistle in it. The shadow of a cloud moved quickly across the grassy slopes at the foot of the mountains.

"Bad weather coming," said John. "We'll be home just before it."

The horses seemed nervous in this wide open place. The skin on their shoulders twitched and they jerked into an uncomfortable canter now and then as if they were in a hurry to get home. We did not meet a soul the whole way to Screeb, though we saw a few isolated houses high on the hillside and people moving about near them who stopped to watch us. At that distance they could not possible have recognized us, but they gazed at us intently all the same, showing, I think, how lonely their lives were. How they made a living was a mystery to me, though I saw a few flocks of mountainy sheep and some little black cows.

At Screeb there was a cross, and the road ahead led off to Carna, John said, which was the back of beyond. We turned south again, onto a road even more empty than the one we had left—a high, windy road that seemed to face a world of nowhere. A quarter of a mile farther along, however, a boreen led down off our road into a valley. There was a scrubby wood down there, and a half-ruined house and barn.

"There's Colman's other place," said John, and there was no mistaking the envy in his voice. "Look at it, all gone to rack and ruin. It's a crime to leave land in that condition."

It looked pretty poor land to me, and I could see how the salt winds from the sea would sweep down that desolate valley and burn the green growth off any crops that would have the courage to come above ground. What a country, I thought, to make a living in! But John evidently had different ideas.

"Any decent man would repair that house and put sheep and Kerry cattle and pigs on the land, and grow potatoes and cabbage. It was a fine place once, my father said. Colman's uncle had it, but his children all went to America and his wife died, and then he lost heart and went to America himself, and died shortly afterward."

"No one lives in the house now?" I asked, after a pause to think about this dreary story.

"Not for years. Colman won't let anyone in, though there's a few people would be glad to have it. A story got around that his uncle's ghost haunts it, but I think Colman made that up himself to stop the procession of people that was coming to his door, asking him for it."

The story of a ghost was the last straw. The house and barn and the desolate land had already made such an unpleasant impression on me that I wondered how anyone in his senses would want to live there.

"Why doesn't Colman want the house lived in?" I asked in bewilderment.

"God knows. Meanness, I think, but it may have been some idea he had of living here himself some day. My father told me that Colman finds it hard to be so near his old home since he sold it to Michael Joyce."

I knew this to be true and for a second I pitied him. Immediately afterward I felt only impatience that any grown man should let his affairs be ordered by such foolishness. Yet I was beginning to understand that such people who live on dreams are always the sufferers in the end, in this world and probably in the next.

"We'll go down and have a look around," said John, who had been observing the little settlement in the valley while we were halted on the road above.

The horses did not like the descent. The road was covered in a mixture of gravel and sand, washed down to the stone foundations here and there by the heavy rains of winter. The grassy verge was narrow and treacherous, full of unexpected holes, so that we could not ride on that. Slowly and cautiously the horses felt their way, rolling a little on the stones and with their heads tossing in fright. Low banks at either side were easy to see over, and the lane curved through them several times, to make the descent less steep. At last we came to the end of it, where there was an iron, five-barred gate. John dismounted and swung it back. We rode in and pulled up on a patch of short grass before the house.

It had been a good house once, rather like the two-story farmhouse where I had stopped on my first night out from Galway. Once there might even have been beds of wallflowers and a climbing rose. One could still see the line of stones, which would have been whitewashed then, enclosing flowerbeds that were now thick with grass. The door might once have been painted red. Battered shutters, faintly red too, covered the

windows on both floors. On the grass around us we saw a few shattered slates, but in general the roof was in good enough condition to keep the house fairly dry. The walls were a depressing gray. I could not imagine how anyone would want to live in such a place. The ghost of Colman's uncle seemed to me the best possible tenant.

But John said, "If it were cleaned up, it would make a fine house again."

He shook his horse's reins and walked him across the yard to the far end of the house. Here there was the skeleton of a hay-shed, balanced like an aged heron on too few legs. The framework of its roof had rotted and the beams hung down dangerously, waiting for the next wind to send them hurtling to the ground. Beyond that was the barn we had seen from above, a strongly constructed stone building of the same kind as the house and with the same good slate roof. It had double doors, held shut by a rusty padlock. Spiders' webs covered the hinges and the angles at either side so that we could see at once that the doors had not been opened for a long time.

"Where were the deer kept when they were out here?" I asked.

"I was told that they were loose on the land," John said. "It's fenced all around so that cattle can't wander in and eat the grass. If the fences were bad, the neighbors could have their cattle in here every day and say they found their way in by themselves."

Clearly the problems of Colman and his empty house had been well discussed and all its possibilities investigated.

"There's nothing here," John was saying. "Wherever the deer are, they're not here now. We might as well move on."

While he spoke, the shadow of a cloud moved across the house so that its dark walls took on a threatening look. Now was the moment for the ghost of Colman's uncle to appear. As we rode out of the yard, I could not resist a quick glance back to see if he were standing by the door. There was no one there, of course, but my sudden, nervous jerk had frightened the

155 🖎

horses so that they plunged away from the gate and went up the lane at a sharp trot. Or perhaps they had seen something that was invisible to human eyes, I thought, remembering some of the Christmas ghost stories that were used to liven up a stormy night in my part of the country.

Altogether we were glad to be back on the main road again, facing toward the sea. We could not see it yet but there was a strong taste of salt on the wind, which was blowing harder every moment. The horses seemed to find it exciting. They tossed their heads and did a prancing sidestep whenever a particularly strong gust struck us. Presently, however, they became resigned and trotted along calmly enough.

"I hope the men have put the boats safe," John said. "It's going to be a storm, all right, but not yet."

"How do you know?"

"The wind is from the west, but there are no clouds over the sea. The clouds are high overhead. When you see them massing low down, dark gray below and a strange pale gray above, that means the storm is very near."

This did not happen until several miles farther on, when we had a full view of the sea. It was a grayish white, with every wave churned up by the wind into a mass of foam, terrifying to see even at that distance. We were passing by a few houses now and we could see that all their doors were shut tightly. The donkeys and the hens were cowering in their sheds, and the cattle were gathered in the corners of the fields trying to escape from the wind. As we rode down the hill, the air was filled with the squalling of seagulls.

"A shark hunt today would be fun," I said.

But John looked so horrified at the thought that I was sorry I had said it. Obviously the sea was not a subject for jokes of any kind.

It was easier riding on lower ground, though the wind came directly at us now. I thought of that terrible house of Colman's in its lonely valley, and I wondered how it would be to live there in weather like this. If Colman were to take his wife there, the thin one, how would she survive?

The space in front of Patsy Carroll's door was like a safe harbor when we reached it. His turf shed at one side sheltered it from the wind so that the house door could be left standing open. This was just as well, because the kitchen was full of pipe smoke, through which we could dimly see the faces of the men staring out at us. John had gone silent a mile before we reached the village. This suited me as it gave me time to think how I should behave. I decided to be quiet, to attract as little attention as possible, and let John do all the talking in the hope that I would be accepted again as one of the people.

We slid to the ground, which seemed to heave under our feet, as if we had been at sea. Canyon appeared at the door.

"Ye're welcome back," he said, and came over to inspect his horse, stroking his neck and looking at his hoofs one by one.

"How did he carry you?" he asked me.

"Fine," I said. "He's a great horse."

"He is that," said Canyon.

He hitched the reins to a hook in the wall, where John had already tethered his. The two horses put their noses together and seemed to settle down for a chat. Then we all went into the kitchen.

Canyon led the way. Perhaps the men knew by our faces that we had bad news for them. A moment passed before I could distinguish who was there. The glare outside, somehow intensified by the approaching storm, and the drifting clouds of tobacco smoke in the kitchen had made my eyes water. Then I saw that Patsy was watching us judicially, and that Martin Folan and Mike Gavin seemed uneasy. I looked around for Colman, rather expecting that he would be there, and saw instead John's father, Ned Hernon, and a man whom I remembered having seen on the quay in Salleen—Morgan Curran. He had also rowed out in his currach to see our catch of sharks on my heroic day, and I remembered that he had later asked for a piece of the skin to rub smooth a chair that he was making.

Patsy said softly, "Well, boys. What did ye find at Inish Goill?"

"We found the deer the first morning, safe and well, and some of the men of the place waiting for the tinkers to come and mend their still."

"Which tinkers? The Wards?"

"No, the Burkes."

"I know them well," said Canyon. "They're good craftsmen."

"Go on," Patsy said.

"We stayed with them a while," John said. "We had our breakfast with them. The Burkes were all day on the island. We saw the deer again in the evening." He stopped.

This time it was his father who said, "Were they well then?"

"Fine. Colman Donnelly was there too."

"Colman!"

"Yes. He came when we were looking at the deer. He said he'd like to ride home with us in the evening, and when we said we were staying till the morning, he said we should go at once. We didn't agree to that and we stayed the night, and he woke us at the dawn the next morning—that's this morning."

"But ye didn't come home with him," Patsy said. "Colman reached home three hours ago."

"In the end he said he wouldn't wait, that he was in a hurry. We wanted to go onto the island again, to have one more look at the deer."

"Good boy, good boy."

But everyone sat forward anxiously now as if they knew what was coming. It could not be put off any longer.

"They were gone," said John. "We searched the island from side to side and from end to end, and there wasn't hair nor hide of them to be seen."

A little burst of exclamations greeted this news. Only Patsy was silent. Then the others fell silent too, looking toward Patsy and clearly expecting him to say something wise. He showed no outward sign of excitement.

"Could the deer have broken loose from the island?" he asked. "Was the bridge by chance left in position so that they just walked off?"

"No," said John. "We made sure of that. But in the morning when we went onto the island, there were tracks of the deer all together at the causeway where the bridge was laid, not as if one rambled off first and then another followed, but as if the whole herd had stood there like cows waiting for someone to open the gate for them. And the bridge was taken over to the mainland afterward."

"And Colman didn't wait for you," Ned said softly.

"What brought him that way at all?" Patsy said, looking at each member of the company in turn. "We didn't tell him that the deer were on Inish Goill."

I knew that there was only one thing to do, though I could feel my whole body go limp and weak at the prospect. In a low voice I said, speaking directly to Patsy, "I told him when he asked me. I didn't know it was being kept from him—" My voice trailed away.

Patsy said in a sharp tone I had never heard from him before, "Speak out, if you have something to say. I can't hear you properly."

This time my voice was a hoarse shout, which surprised myself and made all the men stare at me even harder, "I told Colman Donnelly that the deer were on Inish Goill. No one told me not to. He asked me what the island was called and I told him."

"Was that when you went to visit the house?" Canyon asked softly, insinuatingly.

So I had even been seen then, I thought sourly, and I wondered if we were as watchful as this in my part of the country.

"No," I said. "It was not. It was when I went to look at the deer that are left, on Michael Joyce's land."

"And why did you go there?"

159 🖋

"Because I had never seen a herd of deer before," I said, thinking that this sounded very weak.

But Ned Hernon defended me. "Why wouldn't he go to look at the deer? It was a reasonable thing to do. Now, I would think it strange if he didn't go to look at them."

"That's true, indeed," said Martin Folan. I was glad of his agreement, but a moment later I jumped in my skin when he went on, "There's something I want to ask you now, just while we're talking: isn't it a strange thing for a country boy to be going around the world with a tent? Surely only a city boy would want to be out under the weather."

I stammered my answer: "Then I'm a strange country boy. I like it."

"I like it too," John said. "There's nothing strange in that."

Martin looked at me with a calm, half-humorous expression and gave a pull at his pipe. "I was thinking," he said, "that maybe you're not a country boy at all. I was thinking you were maybe a city boy that's letting on to be a country boy."

"Why?" asked Patsy Carroll sharply.

"I don't rightly know why," said Martin. "It's just that there's something a little bit wrong about him. He knows a lot about us now—things that it doesn't suit us to have a stranger know."

"Didn't I say I'd milk Patsy's cow for him when he'd be away?" I said, thinking that this was an unexpected turn of events. "That would be a dangerous offer to make if I wouldn't be able to carry it out."

"He told me he milks a cow every day at home," Patsy said.

"Maybe he was hoping you would be home early enough to milk her yourself," Martin said. "He let me milk her, in the latter end."

"You said you wanted to!" I said furiously. "You said she was crotchety, like—" I stopped just in time.

Patsy asked, "Like what?"

"Like many another cow," I said weakly.

Martin looked rather grateful that I had not repeated his

remark, that Patsy's cow was crotchety like her owner. He said, "It's true. I remember that. I offered to do it."

"If we need proof," said Patsy, "it's ready to our hand. My cow is due to be milked this moment. She's inside in her stable, for I was afraid the wind would blow her away. There's nothing to stop us all from going out with Peter and putting him to milk her."

The others were all delighted with this idea. Patsy stood up and said, "Come on, then. We have serious business on our hands. Take the can, there, and put on a show for us."

I went to the bench by the door and picked up the milk can. There was a drop in it. I poured this carefully into a mug from the dresser and then I scalded the can thoroughly with boiling water from the kettle over the fire. This made a good impression.

Ned said, "You see. No city boy would be as careful with the milk as that."

I took the can, with something of a swagger now to help me to bring off my test, and went out to the stable. The men followed in a little crowd. The cow was standing in the dark stable with her tail toward the door, as cows always do in windy weather. She turned her head to look at me, and the wisp of hay hanging out of the corner of her mouth gave her a somewhat sardonic look.

A tiny stool hung on a nail on the wall. I saw it at once and took it down, glad not to have to kneel on the filthy floor. I arranged it to my satisfaction, placed the can carefully under the cow's udder, and squeezed out a few jets of milk. Then I paused, dipped the thumb of my right hand into the milk in the can, and withdrew it dripping. With this, I signed a cross on the cow's flank, just by her hip bone. Behind me I heard John chuckle. I bent my head and settled down to the delightful task of milking, sending the jets from either hand singing rhythmically into the can.

Then I heard Martin's voice say, "I'll take it all back. He's a country boy, sure enough."

161 ⚓

# ❧ 10

THEY LET ME MILK THE COW dry. Long before I had done, they went back to the kitchen and I was left alone. John hesitated a moment at the stable door and then went away too, unable to resist hearing whatever was coming next.

It seemed that I was reinstated in the men's confidence and this would surely mean that I would learn what they were planning to do next. I remembered that Michael Joyce's mood when I had seen him last had been of anger that his neighbors should feel they had a right to dictate to him. Knowing the slow but sure Irish way of dealing with foreigners, I feared that if he took this attitude, Michael Joyce would get the worst of whatever game was being planned.

For myself I felt properly trapped. Why should it fall to me to make peace between a rich Argentinian farmer and a collection of wild men of the west? They talked of peaceful methods now, but the guns had in fact already been produced once. Who could tell what would come next? In two shakes, I thought, I would walk as fast and as far from the whole boiling lot of them as my good legs would take me.

But this feeling passed. Perhaps the strongest reason for my staying was curiosity. It seemed to me that the whole matter was at a deadlock, and yet I knew that Patsy and Canyon and the rest of them would not be content to leave it so. I could not bear the idea of going through the rest of my life wondering how it had all been solved. And there was the question of my fee, at least half of which I had certainly earned already.

Canyon had said the time had come to write the letters. That was when he had heard that Hugh, the herdsman, had been frightened away. It looked as if a number of moves in the campaign had been planned in advance and were now going to be carried out one by one. Writing letters seemed a rather harmless activity. I hoped I would be allowed to know what was in them, so that I would be able to prepare Michael Joyce.

I finished the milking and placed the can by the door while I hung the stool on the wall again. The cow swished her tail at me but not at all wickedly. Indeed I had become quite fond of her during our short acquaintance and I thought she had been maligned by Martin.

The wind swayed the can in my hand as I crossed to the house. There was a whistle in it now and it no longer came in gusts but in one great roaring sweep. I guessed that it would darken earlier than usual this evening and I planned to use this as an excuse to go out early and put up my tent, and then somehow to sneak away and have a talk with Michael Joyce. I wondered if he would go to the shelter on the hillside on such a windy evening. If he did not, then I would wait until after dark and go to his house; tap on a window, perhaps, and tell him everything that had happened.

I soon found out that I was not going to be able to make my own arrangements. I crossed the kitchen and placed the can of milk on its bench.

Then Patsy said, "There's another thing you can do for us." He looked at me with the same cold eye that he had turned on me before, so that I felt all my senses sharpen as if for danger.

I made no answer but waited for him to go on. I knew that he could not see me as clearly as he would have liked. The lamp was not yet lit as it was much too early, and between the glowering evening light and the pipe smoke, and the occasional puff of smoke that came down the chimney as well, the kitchen was in semi-darkness.

After a moment, Patsy went on, "While you were out milking my cow, we were saying here that you're a well-spoken boy, with a lot of fine ways of talking, as if you have read a fair share of books in your day."

"That's true," I said, wondering what sort of trap this could be. "The teacher at home used to lend me books always."

"And likely enough, we said, that means that you are a master of the pen, too."

I felt like chuckling at this strange way of putting it, but I answered solemnly enough, "I've been told I have a fair hand."

"Then you're the man we need," said Patsy. "John, here, is the last out of school but he has had more practice with a pair of oars than with a pen since then. The rest of us have nearly forgotten how you go about writing a letter—"

"What about all the letters that must be written to America?" I demanded, beginning in a panic to see what was coming. "What about Canyon, here, that has been all over the world?"

"A lot of that is only old talk," said Patsy confidentially, as if Canyon were not watching him rather sheepishly as he spoke. "Canyon has been around the world, but so has every basking shark that comes into Galway Bay, and who would think of asking one of them to write a letter?"

They all laughed heartily at this idea—too heartily, it seemed to me—and they stopped as suddenly as they had begun.

Patsy said, "Even if we could all write like the great Homer, we wouldn't want to do this piece of writing that we have in mind now."

He paused again, but I would not ask him the question he wanted. I knew the answer. After a moment, he gave it. "We want you to write a letter to Michael Joyce, telling him that his deer were taken because we don't like that class of fancy animal hereabouts, eating the grass that God made for sheep and cattle and horses. You can tell him that he'll have to banish what's left of them, and that if he won't there's plenty more we can do to him and his fine house. That must all be put into the king's English, so that we won't appear to be a pack of savages, and it must not be written in the hand of any man of this place."

And that, of course, was the real reason why they wanted me to do it. I did not know what to say. They were all watching me, but calmly as if they thought I should have time to think the proposition over. I knew well that I was not being given a choice, however. Tales I had heard of Connemara came back to my mind, of knifings and other horrors which the people of Leitrim told to show their own superiority over the wild men from the seacoast. What if some of them were true? How dangerous would it be to refuse to do as I was asked? And if my letter were to fall into the hands of the Civic Guards, who would believe that I had written it under duress? I could imagine myself trying to make the Guards believe the story of Michael Joyce offering a prize of a hundred pounds to a boy he had never seen before, for help in getting back his deer. Would Michael Joyce admit to the Guards that he had done such an extraordinary thing? Could I trust him to defend me? I had seen him only once since I had come out to these wild places. Instead of coming home to my mother a hero with a hundred pounds in my pocket, I might have to be rescued by her from the hands of the law.

After a moment, Patsy stood up and went to the corner cupboard for his writing paper, pen, and a bottle of ink. Just as they had led me to the cow to show that I could milk her, now they led me to the table and seated me in front of these things.

Patsy said, "We won't begin with 'Dear Sir' because that would be dishonest. Just start straight off." And he began to dictate the letter.

Martin Folan said in mock admiration, "Look at that! He points the handle of the pen over his shoulder. That's the first thing I remember being told to do."

No one answered. As Patsy's words came out slowly, the

165 ✒

others made appropriately ferocious faces as if Michael Joyce were physically there and they were threatening him and his property in person. It was true that my handwriting had been praised for being clear and round and smooth. Somehow I managed to keep my hand from shaking so that I was able to give a good performance.

When I had finished, Patsy picked up the letter and read it aloud. I tried not to listen, to shut my ears to what seemed to me a wicked thing. And still I knew that it was this same kind of determination that had made the terrible old Irish landlords treat their tenants like fellow human beings, in the end. Stories of those bad old times had been handed down from father to son for generations, so that every man in Ireland—not only in Connemara—knew exactly how to force a landowner to his knees. There were many more shots in the locker still, as I knew: stones through the window in the night, a hayrick or an out-building burned, the housekeeper and the yardman instructed not to work there any more, and worst of all the possibility that the big house itself might be burned down.

While my imagination galloped ahead, the men were all nodding approvingly at the contents of the letter.

"And a fine hand he has, for sure," Patsy said. "Off with you now, and deliver it."

"Why should I?" I demanded furiously. "All this has nothing to do with me. Next thing you'll be ordering me to—"

I stopped, not wanting to give them any ideas that might not have occurred to them already.

"You're the best for it," Patsy said calmly, "the same as you were the best to write the letter. A strange boy can ramble about anywhere—no one will take any notice."

"On a stormy evening?"

Patsy looked a little uncertain, as if he had not expected me to refuse.

Then John said, "I'll go with him. That's fair. It's not right to send him alone."

"Let them go together," said Canyon. "Less notice is taken

of two boys together than of one that would be wandering alone."

Now I began to regret that I had been so quick in protesting. I had wanted an opportunity of seeing Michael Joyce, and I had been foolish in turning it down when it came. Now, escorted by John, it would be almost impossible to get to his house tonight. Patsy was looking rather pleased, and I guessed that he was glad to have John come with me and make sure that I did as I was told. I wondered which of us would be given the letter to carry.

Patsy seemed to have doubts about this too, but after a second's hesitation he handed it to me."

"Put it out of sight," he said. "There's no use in letting everyone know what you're about. And be quick. We have a lot more to do yet."

When we were outside the door, I said to John, "What did he mean by that?"

"They'll have to find the deer now, I suppose," said John. "They left that over while they got the letter written."

"They think Colman Donnelly has them?"

"Yes, and of course threatening Michael Joyce won't be half as good if he finds out we have lost the deer."

Now I remembered that we had not had a chance of saying that we suspected the Burkes of helping Colman to take the deer off the island.

"We'll tell them when we get back," John said.

Out on the road it was an effort to talk. The wind went down our throats, pressed against our chests, held our legs as if it had huge invisible hands. We were facing directly west, into the last of the sunlight. While we were in the village, there was a little shelter, but once we left the houses behind, we were exposed to the full force of the gale. There was a loose stone wall at the upper side of the road, and the light showed whitely through the chinks. Between the wall and the road there was a deep ditch full of tall grass, with a stream in its depths. I was not particularly watching these things. My eyes were on Colman Donnelly's house, so far from its neighbors, four-square to the wind, and looking horribly lonely in the evening light.

Out of the corner of my eye, I saw something move in the ditch. The heavy grass was blown flat by the wind. I seized John's arm and pointed without a word. Together we turned and plunged into the ditch.

It was a Burke child. I knew it immediately, though all the children had looked the same to me. There was the little wiry body and the rabbity face and wild reddish hair. She looked about seven years old but could have been ten. One never knew what age tinker children were, with their small size and old faces. She struggled like a little weasel, wriggling this way and that, but of course we were able to hold her. She glared at us furiously and stuck out her tongue at us.

John said, "Don't bite or I'll slap you."

"I'll get my father after you! He'll cut out your insides, like he did to many another! He'll bury you ten feet deep, the way he always does, and you'll never be found!"

Her accent was extraordinary, unlike the accent of any special place. I knew it for the tinkers' accent, and this as well as the silly threats of her father made me quite sure she was a Burke.

"What are you doing here? Where is your father?" I asked.

Her only answer was to stick out her tongue again.

John said, "You were on your way to Colman Donnelly's. Had you a message for him?"

"Wouldn't you like to know?" But her hand had gone to her head in a quick, involuntary movement.

John said to me, "Hold her hands."

Again she struggled, while he felt in the mass of her tangled hair and found a tiny piece of paper tied to it with string.

"We can't stay here on the side of the road," he said to me. "Where can we take her?"

"Up on the cliff. There's a sort of cave up there. I saw it the first evening."

She made no more effort to get away, but we held her tightly all the same, in case she was hoping to make a sudden bolt for freedom when we would relax. And she did not yell out, as she might have done, but kept as silent as a rabbit does when you catch it.

We had only a short distance to go before we came to the lane that led down to the well. We hurried into this, glad to be out of sight of a chance passerby. Until we came to the well, we walked three abreast, both of us clutching the child. Where the brambles narrowed the path, I went in front and we made the child follow, while John kept his hands on her shoulders from the back. In this way we reached the place where I had climbed the wall on my first evening.

Here the wind almost blew us off our feet. We had to lean against it with all our force, as if we were trying to push open a door which was held from the inside by a giant. There was not a single rabbit to be seen now, and if the seals were singing on the shore, the howls of the wind drowned their voices. As we went higher, the sea came gradually into view. It was so horrible that I had to pause for a second to look at it. The colors were a strange, unhealthy mixture of pale green and white, and it thrashed and leaped about with no pattern that I could see. Sometimes a wave rose up in a little peak, high above the others, but only for a moment before it broke into wild disorder. Perhaps I should not have found it so frightening if I had not so recently been on it in a currach. Now in the brief glance I gave it, I could not prevent my imagination from putting me out there again in one of those terrible boats.

John turned his back on the sea, with a look almost of boredom. The hut delighted him. "This is a fine place. We can keep her here for a month if we like," he said.

At that the child began to struggle again.

John said, "You may as well give that up, for you haven't a dog's chance of getting free of us. If you're quiet, you'll get better treatment."

She glared at us but said nothing. Secretly I was glad she was so tough. If she had begun to cry, I should have had to let her go at once. Perhaps she was pleased with the hut too, because she walked in there and looked around with interest. It was so dim that we could hardly see at first. When we had become accustomed to it, we sat on the stones by the door, putting the little girl on the inner side so that we blocked the doorway. Here we were sheltered from the worst of the wind and our ears were free of some of its noise.

Then at last John unrolled the little paper which he had kept in his hand until now. He held it high, so that the fading daylight made it possible to read the words. Then he handed it to me. It was a very simple message:

"10 powndes now or they excape."

Some of the letters were turned the wrong way around and the writing sloped downwards, so that one could see it had been painfully composed. The meaning was quite clear, however.

"Your father wrote this," John said.

"Wouldn't you like to know?" For good measure she put out her tongue too.

"Where were you going with it? Up to Colman Donnelly?"

"Wouldn't you like to know?" But suddenly she added, "If you don't let me go, my father will turn them loose. How will you like that?"

"What will he turn loose?"

"The queer cows with the branchy horns that you stole from Mr. Joyce. You know well. They'll go out on the mountain and they'll never be seen again. If I don't get home, that's what my father will do."

"Where is your father?"

She began again on her chant: "Wouldn't you like to know? Wouldn't you like to know?"

"Were you going to Colman Donnelly?"

But it was no use asking her questions. In any case, we knew well enough what must have happened—that Burke had agreed on a price with Colman for removing the deer and was wishing now that he had asked for more. It seemed clear too that he must have the deer in his custody still.

I wished that John and I could have a private talk, unheard by the child. There could be no question of this, because if we had left her for an instant, she would have been off down the hill and we would have had no hope of catching her. I understood why she had said, "if I don't get home." Evidently to her as to myself, home was wherever the tent happened to be at the time.

"Where do the tinkers camp when they come to this part of the world?" I asked John.

"A mile back toward Galway, where there's a wide grassy place beside the road."

One glance at the child's face told me that this was where they would be found. She had shrunk back and was glaring furiously from one of us to the other.

I said doubtfully, "Perhaps we should go back there and tell them they'll get the child in return for the deer."

"We couldn't face the whole family," John said.

Immediately the child began again: "My father will cut you up. He'll bury you ten feet deep. That's what he always does. He cuts them up small first—"

It was a kind of boasting chant, and she got up and paraded around the hut while she gave it out: "He'll cut out your lights. He'll cut out your liver. He'll cut out your kidneys. He'll cut out your stomach—"

"Stop that!" John said sharply.

But she raised her voice and went on and on with her litany. We could do nothing to stop her, as we did not wish to hurt her in any way—she seemed so young and small. There was nothing to do but wait until her voice became hoarse, and finally she came to a stop of her own accord.

Then John said, "Her father will come looking for her. It's nearly dark now. I'll go down and wait for him on the road near Colman's place. He'll come alone, very likely. That's

171

what the tinkers always do when they go scouting. Keep a close watch on that little demon while I'm gone."

Though I did not like my task, it looked like being an easy one. She had gone to sit on the ground far back in the hut, where she was almost invisible in the darkness. Only her face and hands showed dimly, quite motionless now. It was nearly night. I sat so as to block the doorway completely, looking downhill where John had gone out of sight at a run. For the moment he seemed to have forgotten the letter I was carrying, which I could feel hard against my skin under my shirt. Perhaps now it would not be necessary to deliver it at all. If things took a new turn, it might be left over for so long that a new one would have to be written. I would make sure that this would not be done by me.

The thought of that letter filled me with sadness. It seemed to me a terrible thing to write those words to a man who had such an honest, decent look about him as Michael Joyce had. I could imagine what his father had been like and how if he had stayed in Connemara he would have resembled Canyon or Ned Hernon or Martin Folan. They should have been friends of Michael Joyce and I could not understand why it had not been so. It seemed likely that no one who had known his father, before he left Ireland, was still living in the neighborhood. I could feel these thoughts leaping about like a linnet in a cage as I tried to work out the possibilities of what was going to happen next. Then I became aware that someone was coming up the hill toward me. Racing, ragged clouds let the moonlight through in flashes. The wind swallowed every sound. The grass was gray-black, covered with shadows. Yet I could see a steadily moving figure, slow but assured, coming toward me. It could be no one but Michael Joyce himself.

I was so pleased that I leaped to my feet with a shout, which was carried away by the wind. He had heard it, however. When he was close enough he said, "A wonderful evening. I love this place in a storm. I wondered if you would come. Last evening I was here and there was no sign of you."

I did not move from my position but kept well inside the entrance. He sat on the stone beside me.

"I've been up the country for a couple of days," I said. "I've seen the deer. They were on that island, Inish Goill. It's on Lough Corrib."

"I never thought of that," he said. "Are they well and healthy?"

"They were when I saw them." I said. "But they have been moved. Colman Donnelly paid a tinker to take them away."

173 🖋

"Colman Donnelly!"

"Yes. He wants to keep them."

"I'd never have thought of him as a thief."

"He doesn't think of himself that way either," I tried to explain. "He just thinks this is his chance of getting something for nothing. They all think of deer as wild animals that anyone can catch. And he's sorry he sold you the land, of course."

"I've been mighty sorry sometimes that I bought it."

"Colman is an oddity," I said. "The others are not like him. They're furious with him for interfering."

"Are they suspicious of you?"

"No. Not at all. In fact they're trusting me more than I like. They want me to join in everything." I could not bring myself to mention the letter.

"Are the deer safe?"

"So far as I know," I said. "The tinker has them somewhere. A boy who was with me until a short while ago is gone down to find that tinker and threaten him until he gives them up.'"

"You mean he's going to get the men of the village to threaten him?"

"No. And it's much more than this village. Everyone for miles around seems to be mixed up in it. Patsy Carroll is the leader."

"What is he going to threaten him with? One boy alone?"

"We have one of that tinker's children," I said reluctantly. "John is gone down to meet the father and tell him he can have her back if himself and Colman Donnelly give back the deer."

"Where is the child?"

"Right here beside us," I said.

"God help us! Here in the hut?"

"Yes."

He stood up and moved into the hut. I turned to peer into the darkness. That was her chance. She must have been right behind my shoulder, as close as she dared, to hear everything we said. She gave a spring like a young goat and was outside in a second. There she remained, dancing up and down, shrieking like a seagull: "My father will get you! He'll cut you up in slices! He'll bury you ten feet deep! I'll tell on you! I'll tell them all on you!"

And then she flashed away down the hill, darting from side to side as a rabbit does when the dogs are after it, and quickly disappeared among the shadows.

I took one step to follow her and stopped immediately. One might as well try to catch a fish that has slipped off the hook.

Michael Joyce called out, "Don't go after her! Let her go. You couldn't drag her back here."

This was true, indeed. It had been all right the first time, but I could not imagine myself hauling her by force up the hill again and imprisoning her in the cave.

"I'll go down," I said after a moment, "but I won't try to catch her. Perhaps John has already met her father. Perhaps he knows where the deer are now."

"I'll go with you."

"No! They must not see us together."

"The child will tell them," said Michael Joyce. "She said she would. It's her most convenient revenge. We'll try to find your friend before she does."

We seemed to sail down the hill before the wind, which had made every step on the way up so difficult. Indeed at times I thought I was going to be knocked forward by it and ridden over as one might be by a stampede of horses. In the lane it was quieter. Michael Joyce moved as fast and as easily as I did, though I would have thought that middle age would have made him stiff and slow. We trotted past the well and out onto the road without seeing any sign of the child. A light showed now in Colman Donnelly's house. I thought then, as I have often thought since, how calmly a light can shine from a house where strange and terrible things are happening. I have never since that time looked up a side road at a lighted cottage window and envied the peaceful life inside.

In single file we ran up the lane to the house, keeping to the grassy edge for quietness. There was no sign of the child. I thought it likely that she had avoided the road and had taken a way across the fields. If she had been anywhere near us, she would not have resisted shouting jeers and threats at us. She was so furious at her captivity that I did not think she would hide in the ditch now as she had done before. Guesswork in the dark was making my head spin. Almost as if I were present, I could see the scene in Patsy Carroll's kitchen when the child would rush in and pour out her story about me. They would believe her at once, of course. I could feel myself shrink with shame at the thought of what they would say about me, and I felt another terror too at the thought of what they would do.

At Donnelly's house I was surprised to find the door standing open. In the few days that I had been here, it had always been genteelly shut, unlike every other house in the village and the district around. The parlor door was open too, and the light from it streamed out into the narrow hall. I reached it in two steps and looked in.

Mrs. Donnelly, the thin one, was sitting there alone. She was leaning back in one of the stiff armchairs, so still and white that I thought she had fainted. Then she opened her eyes and saw me. She looked rather relieved, but in a moment, when Michael Joyce appeared behind me, she covered her face with her hands.

"Where is Colman?" I asked. "What has happened?"

"He's gone with the boy from Salleen and a tinker."

"A tinker!"

"That's what they said." She looked at me, horrified at the memory of it. "They said such extraordinary things—that Colman stole Mr. Joyce's deer. Can that be true?"

"Not quite true," I said gently, "but there's something in it."

"And the tinker said a lot about money and about being afraid of going to jail, and that Colman would have to go with him."

"Colman won't go to jail," said Michael Joyce. "Did you know nothing of what was going on?"

"Nothing at all. The people don't talk to me much. I knew the deer had disappeared but I never heard what had happened to them. I wanted to go to the village and talk to the people there and find out, but Colman said not to. He said they don't like strangers and they would tell me nothing. They look so friendly—but I had to do as he said."

"Where have they gone? Colman and the boy and the tinker?"

"Up to the Screeb farm. They took the two horses—only a few minutes ago."

"To the Screeb farm! That's where they are, then."

I made for the door at once but Michael Joyce blocked my way. A full five minutes he delayed while he talked to Mrs. Donnelly and made her go into the kitchen and put on the kettle for some tea, and reassured her over and over again that nothing would happen to Colman.

When we were out in the lane again at last, he said with a chuckle, "Here am I all my life and I could get no woman to care for me. Isn't it wonderful to think that a half-man like Colman would be able to rouse such anxiety in any woman?"

"She's lonely." I said. "And after all she's only a half-woman."

He gave a shout of laughter. Then he said, "She said nothing about the tinker's child."

"Should I go back and ask her?"

"No. There's no time. Where is this Screeb farm?"

"A few miles up the hill. I was there only this morning, but the deer were not there then, that we could see."

"Who was with you?"

"The boy from Salleen, John Hernon."

"Will you know your way there again?"

"Yes."

"Then we'll go at once and get horses."

# ❦ 11

SO THERE I WAS AGAIN, riding up the long road to Screeb on a horse whose acquaintance I had made only a few minutes before. He was a tall bay, more like the hunters in my part of the country than any horse I had seen in Connemara. Michael Joyce's was black and just as handsome. We rode knee to knee because the horses liked it that way. They had been in adjoining loose-boxes in Michael Joyce's stable yard. I wondered how many horses he had in there. While we were saddling ours, I heard hoofs knock on cobblestones as several others heard ours being taken out.

The wind seemed to trouble our horses a great deal, as if they were not accustomed to it, and they tossed their heads against it angrily. As we went higher, it became stronger, and I understood how nothing but rough grass and furze would grow there, since in winter especially this wind would be laden with bitter salt. We had light from the moon, which seemed to be sliding dizzily through the hurrying clouds. I could not look at it. In any case we were too much occupied with gazing ahead for a sign of Colman and John and the tinker to have eyes for anything else.

"It's a pity you delayed to talk to Mrs. Donnelly," I said. "We'll never catch up with them now."

"We couldn't have left her in that condition," he said.

We kicked at our horses with our heels and made them go faster, but we were afraid to canter on account of the dim light. Also, the road occasionally took a swoop downward before climbing again, and in these places we had to slow to a walk.

At last I said, "We're coming near it. There's the valley. The house and barn are where the dark patch is."

No light showed down there. Now suddenly the moon sailed out into a sky blown clean of clouds. The wind made a thundering noise which filled the air and the very ground under our feet as if we were riding across a volcano in eruption. I hated the feeling of smallness that it gave me. We might have been two ants crawling on a rock for all our importance in that huge world.

"They are down there already," Michael Joyce said.

At the turn down to the house, we reined in and sat there watching. A point of light had appeared in one of the lower windows, showing through a crack in the ancient shutter. Now it disappeared for a minute and then reappeared at the open door, much bigger, swinging in the hand of whoever was carrying it.

"A lantern," I said softly, as if we were near enough to be heard.

It moved along the front of the house, in the direction of the barn. Slowly we rode down the lane, this time in single file, until we reached the gate. Here we slid to the ground, opened the gate and went through, walking stiff-legged and leading our horses. Their hoofs made no sound on the thick grass that grew everywhere, where once there had probably been a gravel sweep. I remembered seeing a hitching post by the house wall, and very quickly we tethered the horses there by the reins.

Suddenly Michael Joyce said, "The lantern! Why do they need a lantern?"

"The deer must be in the barn now," I said, surprised that

he had not thought of this at once, since no lantern would be needed outside tonight.

"In the barn!"

He began to run, and I followed as best I could, stumbling over some obstruction which lay hidden in the grass and which sent me rolling to the ground. I was up at once and after him, hearing him shout out something at the top of his lungs. He reached the barn door. There was no sign of the lantern nor of it's bearer. He flung the door open and stood still. A moment later I was beside him, gazing at one of the most extraordinary sights I have ever seen.

The barn was illuminated by the gray-blue light of the moon, which streamed in through a row of glassless windows high up on the eastern side. The lantern gave a weak yellow glow. It was enough to show us the bodies of the three does lying huddled in a corner, streaming with blood. In front of them, facing us, stood the buck with his head high and his huge antlers moving slowly from side to side. John was bending over the dead does. Burke had shrunk back against the leaf of the door which Michael Joyce had opened. I guessed that he would have been outside and away if we had not blocked him. Colman, holding the lantern, was standing still in the middle of the floor, looking as if he had lost the power of movement.

The buck took a single slow step forward and flourished his antlers. He stopped and then came forward again, with a prancing step, very pretty to see, moving his head gracefully.

Michael Joyce let out a yell which ended in a wail. "Run, for God's sake, you fool!"

The tinker darted outside. John came flying to the doorway, only Colman did not move, but stayed there as if he were fascinated by the buck's slow, elegant movements.

Now the buck took one step more and then bent his head and gently poked Colman in the stomach with his antlers. Colman held the lantern wide, as if to save it from damage, but still he did not move. Michael Joyce leaped forward, knocking Colman aside with his shoulder, and seized the buck's antlers as they came down for a second thrust. I ran and took Colman by the arm and pulled him to the door. He was like a sleep-walker, dragging each foot so that it was almost like having to carry him.

When we reached the open door, I turned to see what was happening behind me. Now Michael Joyce had the buck's ant-lers grasped in his two hands, and a sort of horrible wrestling match was going on between them. It would almost have looked like a game, if the dead bodies of the gored does had not been there to prove how wickedly bloodthirsty the buck was.

"A stick!" I shouted to John. "Get a stick, somewhere."

He ran outside. In despair I wondered where one would find a stick in this wilderness where no trees grew. I moved in behind Michael Joyce, abandoning Colman for the moment in relative safety. The buck's hoofs were still moving in a sort of rhythmic dance. Michael Joyce was a huge man, strong enough to throw a bull, I would have thought. Yet that fragile-looking beast with his slim legs and light body seemed to be a match for him. They swayed and swung together. I could see the sweat glistening on Michael Joyce's face, and a dark stain on his wrist showed that the sharp antlers had cut the skin of his hands.

"A stick," he said, panting.

"John is gone for one."

"This fellow is a murderer."

I could not have helped him with what he was doing. No weapon of any sort could be seen in the barn—not a spade, nor a pitchfork, nor even a length of rope. On an inspiration I took off my sweater and began to slap at the buck's heels with it. This foolish-seeming activity had a marvelous effect. For one moment it interrupted the intensity of the buck's attack. That was enough for Michael Joyce. In a second he had got to the animal's side and was bending his neck backwards. At once the buck was helpless, and with a quick, powerful twitch he was thrown to the ground.

Michael Joyce stepped back, shaking the blood from his hands. The buck was scrambling to his feet. We started for the door, where Colman still stood foolishly staring. And there came John with a sweeping brush, worn down so that it looked like the beard of an old goat, but with a fine, strong handle.

Without a word, Michael Joyce seized it and brandished it high, and then brought it down with force on the side of the buck's nose. We leaped aside as he came charging through the open doorway. The horses whinnied in terror at the strangeness of that bounding figure. Other horses answered nearby. Burke, whom I had thought would by now be half a mile away, opened the gate of the yard. The buck went galloping through, and we could hear him plunging off up the hill.

Then suddenly we were surrounded. In my shocked state, it was a moment before I realized who the people were and why there were so many of them. Martin Folan and Canyon Lee and Patsy Carroll were there, as well as Mike Gavin and Ned Hernon and Morgan Curran. One by one I recognized them. I was so weary now that I hardly cared what they thought of me. All around me I could hear angry growls, with my name repeated often, but in that moment when the buck went galloping free up the hill, I had felt my fighting spirit go with him.

John it was who knew what to do. The men were crowded in the doorway of the barn, blocking our way out. Over by the gate I could see Burke like an old scarecrow blown about by the wind. He seemed to hesitate for a moment and then he simply disappeared. I suppose he dropped out of sight into a ditch, or leaped over the bank and went crawling away at the far side of it, but in the patchy light it seemed to me as if he had vanished into the air.

John said loudly, "Come in, all, and see the deer!" He took the lantern out of Colman's hand and walked to the back of the barn. I stayed in the shadows by the door, not wanting to look again at such ugliness. I could hear by their murmurs that it was having its effect on the men.

"The buck slaughtered them all—drove them into the corner and gored them to death. And he was going to do the same to Colman only that Mr. Joyce got between them, pushed Colman aside, and threw the buck."

"God help us!" said Canyon. "There's a slaughter!"

No one else said a word. At last Michael Joyce said quietly, "It's no one's fault that they're dead, really. The tinker didn't know that you can't shut a buck into a small place because he'll kill everything and everyone he can get his horns into. And the storm tonight, the noise of the wind, probably excited him. They're strange animals. One needs to know how to handle them."

The men looked very downcast and I guessed what they were thinking—that whatever about handling deer, it was common knowledge that one should not steal a neighbor's property.

Patsy Carroll was the first to recover. "There's no good in staying here," he said. "We could go into the house, but I'm thinking there wouldn't be much comfort in it. Down at my place we'll have a fire at least, and a barrel of porter."

They only wanted wind of the word. They left that barn so quickly that they were tripping over each other's heels in their hurry. No one looked back.

Patsy kept his head, and most of his usual calm way of talking as he said, "Mr. Joyce, let you ride with me and we'll be conversing on the way down the hill."

They rode out in front, and we all mounted our horses and followed in pairs like a little army. The storm had died down, and the road and the bare hills were all white with moonlight. John and I made sure to get to the back of the cavalcade, so that we could talk to each other in low voices.

"You never saw the child again?" I began as soon as we were moving.

"No, but she did her work well. She must have gone straight to Patsy's place and broken the news. I saw her father the moment I got down to the road. He was hanging around near Donnelly's boreen, waiting for the child to come back with the ten pounds. I put the fear of God in him in short time. I told him we'd have him in jail for life if he wouldn't give up those deer. That was what frightened him. He only laughed when I told him we had the child. He said, 'You won't have her long, if I know her.' "

"That was true for him," I said. "No one could hold her. So you both went to Donnelly's."

"Yes. Colman didn't want to come at first, until he saw how frightened the tinker was, and his wife, poor soul, having a fit for fear he'd be put in jail, too."

"Mr. Joyce told her that won't happen," I said, and I described our visit to Donnelly's house.

"She must have got a worse fright when Patsy and the rest of them arrived," John said. "And she did us a service when she sent them after us."

It was a joy to me to see Patsy Carroll and Michael Joyce riding side by side. Surely if they could spend an hour together in Patsy's kitchen, an understanding would grow between them which would end the foolish opposition of the people to his coming to live in the big house. Foolish it was, for anything less like an old-time landlord than Michael Joyce it would be hard to imagine.

One problem was solved when we reached Colman Donnelly's house. I had been imagining how his presence in Patsy's kitchen would make everyone uneasy and slow the talk, so that perhaps after all no good would come of it. But when we reached his own lane, Colman reined in his horse and said loudly to the whole company, "I'd best be going home to tell my wife what happened. Good night to you all."

When he had left us, the whole line broke into a fast trot in their eagerness to reach Patsy's kitchen and settle down to discuss the evening's doings.

In the end, it was the Scotsman that got all the blame, by common consent. He was a convenient object for it, being gone out of the district for good, and it was true that he was one of the main causes of the suspicion that had quickly developed against Michael Joyce among his neighbors. When Canyon had started up the avenue to pay a visit of welcome in the first days, the Scotsman had sprung out from nowhere, asked his name and business, and said he thought Mr. Joyce was busy. That was enough. No one had ever before suggested that a visit from Canyon might not be an honor. As a traveled man, he had naturally been the ambassador of the whole area. It was a bad start, and within a few days a decision had been taken against Michael Joyce. This was all the easier since he was now the owner of all the good land in the neighborhood.

"But we never knew your father was a Joyce from Casla," Patsy said. "If we had known that in the beginning, things might have been a bit different."

And a discussion began about Michael Joyce's ancestors. No one looked at me nor took any notice of me. At first I was rather pleased at this, but as time went on I began to dislike the fact of being so completely ignored. A remark would be addressed to the man on my right and on my left, but I might have been invisible for all the heed they gave me.

At last I could stand it no longer. I stood up and went to the door as if to take some fresh air, and a moment later I had slipped outside. Hot and angry, I walked along the road to the west. What right had these people to treat me so uncivilly? Only for me, at this moment a feud would be raging which might easily have ended in murder. Because of me, friendship had begun between Michael Joyce and his neighbors, a thing that had seemed impossible only a few days ago. I had earned my money, and as soon as I would have collected it from Michael Joyce, I would leave this district for good and never come near it again.

So, raging and fuming, I walked a mile or more, and I might be walking still only that I heard the sound of hoofs on the road behind me. I stopped by the side of the road and waited for the horseman to pass by. But it was John, and he reined in when he saw me.

"Where would you be going?" he asked.

"It's all one to me," I said, "so long as I don't go back to that house."

"Hold on!" said John. "They sent me out to get you." He gave a short laugh. "You were no sooner gone out of the door than they began to argue about you—to ask how you came to be here, how you came to know Michael Joyce, why he picked on you to do his spying for him."

"Spying!"

"What else was it? They were cross in the beginning, but then they began to remember the sharks. And then they thought of the bold Colman Donnelly, one of their own, that wasn't satisfied to play in with them but wanted to steal the deer for himself, and they began to think there was a lot of things in the whole story that a man wouldn't like to be telling his grandchildren. And the end of it was that they said you had done the best for everyone, and they're sorry they looked so black at you, and would you come back now and drink a glass with them."

"Who said that?"

"Canyon, of course. But Sarah John and Maggie Tom are there now too, and Sarah said boys are not getting porter while she's under the roof, so they're making tea, and Maggie went home for a new currant cake she has, and please, Peter, come back with me now and we'll all be the best of friends."

During this speech all of my anger was gradually disappearing. I could hardly believe that only a few minutes before I had been swearing never to lay eyes on any of them again.

I rode back to Patsy's in style, pillion behind John, and found a great party in progress. This time I was received like a hero, which I felt was only my due. For most of the night we talked, going into every possible aspect of the story. The men asked many questions about the breeding of deer, and I thought it likely that in future times they would not be so uncommon in that part of the world. No one thought of sleep, least of all Michael Joyce. He looked so contented now, it did my heart good to look at him. He and Canyon seemed to have become great friends, and I could hear them talking about the strange places they had seen in the New World.

I slept in Patsy's kitchen and was surprised to find that I would have preferred my tent. The pipe smoke and the turf smoke had poisoned the tightly shut room, which made me wish for the wind blowing in and around me as I had been used to have it in the last few days. However, Patsy had obviously felt he was honoring me by allowing me to stay, and with our newly mended friendship I could not have thought of refusing.

When the little house was quiet and Patsy had had time to go to sleep, I took out the threatening letter which was still inside my shirt. Without unfolding it, I buried it in the ashes that covered the fire. A few minutes later I saw it blaze up and disappear. I was very glad to see it go.

Toward morning I got up and cautiously opened the door, and the clear air, laden with the fresh smells of grass and wallflowers, filled the kitchen. The storm was over, and the birds were shrieking their morning chorus on the roof and in the little apple tree that grew against the end of the house. I stayed for a few minutes to breathe in all this sweetness, and then I went back to bed and slept until Patsy woke me. I thought he would be angry about the open door but all he said was, " 'Tis true that you're fond of fresh air. It's a peculiar taste for a country boy."

That was the end of the story of the herd of deer. Michael Joyce worked hard on me to stay with him altogether, but though I was very much tempted, I could not bring myself to do it then. He helped me to write the difficult letter to my mother, which explained something of what I had been doing, and that I would spend the rest of the summer with him minding deer instead of with my cousin minding sheep. When I left him at last, it was with my fee in my pocket and a promise that I would come back every summer. His house was full of books, he said, and it would take a healthy man several years to read them all.

I did not need this inducement. Already I had become attached to this part of the world, and to the slow-moving people who lived there, and I knew that this would continue so as long as I lived. And that is how it has turned out.